IN DUE TIME

HOUSTON, WE HAVE A KLUTZ!

by Nicholas O. Time

Simon Spotlight

New York   London   Toronto   Sydney   New Delhi

SIMON SPOTLIGHT

An imprint of Simon & Schuster Children's Publishing Division

1230 Avenue of the Americas, New York, New York 10020

This Simon Spotlight hardcover edition November 2016

Copyright © 2016 by Simon & Schuster, Inc. Text by Sheila Sweeny Higginson. Cover illustration by Stephen Gilpin.

All rights reserved, including the right of reproduction in whole or in part in any form.

SIMON SPOTLIGHT and colophon are registered trademarks of Simon & Schuster, Inc.

For information about special discounts for bulk purchases, please contact Simon & Schuster Special Sales at 1-866-506-1949 or business@simonandschuster.com.

Designed by Jay Colvin. The text of this book was set in Adobe Garamond Pro.

Manufactured in the United States of America 1016 FFG

10 9 8 7 6 5 4 3 2 1

ISBN 978-1-4814-7237-1 (hc)

ISBN 978-1-4814-7236-4 (pbk)

ISBN 978-1-4814-7238-8 (eBook)

Library of Congress Control Number 2016945240

CHAPTER	TITLE
1	Being Graceless

I can feel it coming. That awful feeling you get when you know someone is talking about you and that they're not saying nice things. Do you know that feeling? If you do, I'm really sorry, because honestly, it's the worst. The sad thing is, I've been getting that feeling more and more lately. And I'm not really a conspiracy-theorist kind of girl. So I'm sort of thinking people really *are* talking about me more. And by people, I mean my fellow students at Sands Middle School.

"Grace, watch out for that . . . ," Matt warns me.

"Step," he is about to say. But I miss the bottom step before Matt can get the word out. I fall flat onto my face and my books go flying. Again.

"That's the third time this week!" I moan.

"Maybe your feet are still stuck in 1951," Luis whispers.

"Or your balance," Matt chimes in, smiling.

I hope you don't get the wrong impression about Luis and Matt. They're totally great guys, and I've been friends with them forever. They'd do anything for me, and I would for them. But it's easier for them to laugh off an uncomfortable situation, like watching me fall on my face, than to deal with real feelings. Which I know is their way of trying to make it all seem not so bad. And it wouldn't be, except for the crowd of other kids who just saw my free fall.

I try to get myself back up to standing again without making too much of a scene, but since that involves my foot sliding across one of the books I've just dropped, in the middle of lifting myself to a standing position . . . Well, you can imagine it's not a very pretty picture. Good thing I didn't wear a skirt today.

And maybe Luis has a point. Maybe my feet *are* stuck in 1951. Because you would think that after having the kind of once-in-a-lifetime, mind-blowing experience like the one we just had, I'd have come out differently on the other side of it. A little wiser . . . a little more polished . . . and definitely with the ability to put one foot in front of the other and not trip over it. Except in my case, not.

I can't tell you too much about it, time-traveler code of honor and all, but if you're wondering where all this talk about 1951 comes from, let me give you a hint. It involves a magical book, a librarian, Matt's grandfather, and a trip through time that I would have never believed possible. Confused? Join the club. I'm still not sure that it even *was* possible. But more on that later. Right now, back to the awful feeling.

I don't even have to guess that the buzzing murmurs from the crowd mean they're all talking about me, because it's so obvious that they are. They're not even trying to hide it anymore. I can feel my cheeks burning as Matt and Luis hand me the books they have just collected from across the hall floor. It's beyond embarrassing.

"Move it, klutz," Jason Coppola says with a laugh as he pushes past me, almost causing me to toss my books again.

"What's up, Graceless?" Jessica Flannery laughs from in front of her locker.

"What's your problem, Jessica?" Matt snarls.

You gotta love that boy. I know Matt thinks that I don't know kids have been calling me Graceless since second grade. He's sweet like that. But if I didn't know about that nickname, they could call me Clueless, too. It's not that big of a leap of creativity, really. Grace—Graceless, I'm not impressed.

I *am* embarrassed to be living up to their stupid nickname, though. And my heart feels like it's being squeezed in someone's hand when I notice that in the midst of Jessica Flannery's giggling fan-girl group is Morgan Stevens.

I've known Morgan since the fourth grade, when we were both into the same fantasy book series: DragonDamsels. We used to spend hours in our rooms talking about the damsels, we'd doodle in each other's notebooks, and we even took an oath to never tell anyone but each other our DragonDamsel names. (Sorry, I can't do it. Even if she is laughing at me now, I will never break that oath.) Last year when Morgan was having trouble in history class, we spent hours together in the library reviewing Roman Empire facts. She ended up getting an eighty-nine in the class with my help. As Shakespeare would say, *Et tu,* Morgan? You too?

So the feeling—that feeling—well, it's a little hard to hide right now. I can feel the tears collecting in the ducts underneath my eyes, so I tell Matt and Luis I need to stop at the bathroom before I go to class. All I have to say is "girl stuff" and they scurry away as if I just told them I had the measles.

Once I pull myself together, the rest of the morning isn't very eventful. All of my teachers are happy to see me—they always are. I'm happy to have schoolwork to focus on, and even if my classmates aren't as happy about the work as I am, at least it keeps them busy.

I will admit, there are a couple of times when I think I hear my name, or my nickname, whispered in the back of the classroom, but I could be wrong, so I am choosing to ignore it.

Until lunchtime, that is. The thing with being super clumsy, which I have no problem admitting that I am, is that the more you think about it and the more you try to overcome your natural tendencies, the more anxious you become about them. And then that anxiety fuels those tendencies like anger fuels the Hulk and well . . . clumsy to the infinitesimal power is the result.

I know the anxiety's going to start the second I step foot into the lunchroom. I try to do some of the strategies I practiced with my dad. I stop, take a deep breath, and keep my eyes focused on the goal.

The goal is: Grab a lunch tray, choose the least offensive food offerings, and carry it to a table, hopefully one where no one who would be whispering about me is sitting. I tackle the first two steps successfully. Even though beef patties aren't my favorite item, they are a lot more edible than the cardboard-flavored pizza that is baking under the cafeteria's hot lamps. I grab a side salad and fill a little cup up with dressing. Sometimes I slip and miss the little cup, but today there is not even a drip down the side. I sigh with relief.

I'm feeling pretty good, so I keep my eyes focused on my target—an empty table—as I walk past Jessica Flannery. I hear something squish underneath my feet, but I am determined to just get to the table and ignore everything that might distract me. Until I hear Jessica shriek.

"Way to go, Graceless," Jessica moans. "You just got ketchup all over my new boots. Thanks a lot!"

I look down and see that she's right. The squishing sound came from a ketchup packet I'd inadvertently stepped on. I mean, it's not really my fault, because I wasn't the one who put the ketchup on the floor, but I don't think Jessica's going to buy that argument.

"I'm sorry, Jessica," I say. "I didn't see the packet there. Is there something I can do to help?"

"Yeah," Jessica says. "Stay away from me. As far away as you can get."

The girls at Jessica's table all roll their eyes and giggle.

"My mom is going to freak when she sees this,"

Jessica tells them. "These boots cost *mucho dinero*, as my Spanish teacher would say. A lot of money!"

Jessica's words, and the giggling, echo in my head as loud as an ambulance siren. I look over at Morgan and her eyes quickly dart away from mine. Forget Graceless. I'm *Hopeless*!

I take my tray over to the empty table and slump down onto the bench. I don't feel like eating anymore. Matt and Luis come and sit next to me. If they saw what happened with Jessica, they're doing a good job pretending they didn't. Matt starts to talk about his big game later that afternoon. It's time for me to tune out.

I settle into my seat and realize that I feel so alone. It's strange. I have two great friends sitting on either side of me. I'm in a lunchroom filled with laughing kids whom I've had good times with in the past. But right now, in this moment, I am like my pet snail, Swifty, during the winter— trapped alone inside my shell.

"Earth to Grace! Are you in there?" Luis calls into my ear.

"I'm here." I smile at him. "I just have a lot on my mind."

"Sure you do." Luis laughs. "Or you just find Matt's baseball talk as boring as I do."

"Hey!" Matt protests. "I thought you guys like baseball now!"

"We do," I tell Matt.

"So come check out my game after school today," Matt says. "I'm pitching, you know."

"Not today, Matt," I say. "I'm going to go home and read. I'm *really* into this new book."

"Oh yeah," Luis says. "Which one?"

"Um . . . I can't remember the title right now. I left the book home," I say, flustered, because I can't even think right now.

"Right," Matt says disbelievingly. "No worries, Grace. We're here if you need us."

"Always," I say. "I know."

That afternoon when the dismissal bell rings, I keep my head down as I scurry toward my locker and quickly pack up my books. I just want to blink my eyes, disappear from Sands Middle School, and reappear safe inside my own bedroom, but I don't have any magical books to transport me at the moment. It's up to me, and only me, to get from my locker, through the crowded halls, and out the school doors without any major mishaps. Fingers crossed.

I'm actually doing a pretty good job of zigzagging through the daily throng of middle schoolers without being noticed. Now I just have to get past the library and down the stairway, and them home free! Except . . .

THWACK! CRASH! BANG!

I'd like to ignore the commotion coming from inside the library, but given my recent history in there, I just can't. And when Ms. Tremt, our school librarian, appears at the door, her usually neat hair looking like a bird's nest and her crazily colorful scarf almost falling off her neck, I know my dreams of getting to my room are doomed.

"Is everything okay?" I ask Ms. Tremt.

"It will be, Grace," she replies. "But at the present time, sadly, it is not."

"What's not?" I ask. "Maybe I could help?"

Ms. Tremt takes a step closer to me and then leans her face toward mine. She stares into my eyes, her nose nearly touching my nose. If it were anyone else, I'd be busting out laughing right now, but it's Ms. Tremt, and she's looking so super serious that I'm getting a little nervous.

"You know, Grace," Ms. Tremt finally says, so close that I can feel the breath she takes with each word. "I believe you may be able to."

She begins explaining the problem to me. It involves Ms. Tremt's glowing, magical pen. I know that I said before that I am bound by the time-traveler code of honor, but if I don't explain this, you're going to be totally lost, so here it goes. . . .

Matt, Luis, and I found out the truth about Ms. Valerie Tremt not very long ago. The first clue was her name. Check it out—if you unscramble the letters, they also spell out "time traveler." And that's the truth. Our librarian, who seems a little zany with her wacky colorful scarves and her instinctual ability to put exactly the right book into each of our hands, is actually a time traveler. Or rather, a time-travel facilitator, at the very least. Because while I haven't actually seen Valerie Tremt travel through time, she was the reason that Matt, Luis, and I got to travel back to 1951. Are you following me? Good, because I know it's a lot.

The way we got to time travel was by using Ms. Tremt's special magical pen to write in *The Book of Memories*. It's like this weird portal to the past (and maybe future, who knows?), but it's also an actual book, and you need to "sign it out" using the magical pen to write in the details of your destination. You know, time, place, that kind of stuff.

Anyway, right now Ms. Tremt cannot find the pen and she has searched high and low, but sometimes she can be a little scattered, so I suggest that we do a systematical search again. I may be clumsy in my movements, but my brain is a nimble beast.

Ms. Tremt, however, seems to be really flustered at the moment. She keeps mumbling something that sounds like, "tim-rah-vel-teer." I'm not sure if that is some secret time-traveling chant, or a foreign language phrase, but the way Ms. Tremt is saying it gives me the feeling that it's not a good thing.

"Ms. Tremt," I interrupt. "We need to focus.

Now, think hard. Where is the last place you remember using the pen?"

Ms. Tremt starts mumbling to herself again, and I'm sure she says "Patrick" and "Luis" in there, but she clearly doesn't want to tell me the details, so I decide we'd better try another strategy. It's one my mom taught me.

"Let's divide the room into levels," I suggest. "We can start with the bottom level first, in case it fell on the floor or rolled off a table, and then move up from there."

"An excellent plan," Ms. Tremt agrees.

We split up, head to opposite sides of the room, and get on our hands and knees. Crawling around the library floor isn't exactly how I'd planned to spend my afternoon, but at least there's no danger of me tripping.

It turns out there is danger, though, and it's hiding behind the historical fiction bookshelf. That's where I find this massive grumpy guy, looking like he's walked out of the pages of *Viking Explorers*. He's got a thick, furry red beard, a giant sword and shield, and a winged metal hat.

"Oh great, Erik," Ms. Tremt moans.

"As in, 'Erik the Red'?" I ask.

"The one and only," Ms. Tremt replies.

The Norwegian explorer looks like he's a little lost, and not very happy about it. He grumbles and growls and knocks over stacks of books and topples tables and chairs.

"I think he's looking for his Viking warriors," Ms. Tremt whispers.

"Are they here too?" I ask.

"They don't seem to be." Ms. Tremt sighs. "Which is a relief. But this . . . this is a very big problem, Grace."

"I'm starting to see that," I agree. "Can you send him back?"

"Not without my pen," Ms. Tremt says.

Erik is making a big mess, and it's more doubtful than ever that we'll actually find Ms. Tremt's pen. So my logical brain starts to buzz again.

"We need a plan B," I tell Ms. Tremt. "He looks like a powerful guy. Maybe you could put him to work here."

"He's a little too rough with the books," Ms. Tremt says doubtfully.

"I wasn't thinking he'd make a great librarian." I laugh. "But he looks like he'd be a good gym teacher. Look at the way he's using his sword and shield—I bet the girls lacrosse team could learn a thing or two from him."

"I like the way you think, Grace." Ms. Tremt smiles. "If I can't find the pen by tomorrow morning, Sands Middle School may have a new substitute coach on the lacrosse field."

"And in the meanwhile?" I ask.

"I'd better start researching some Viking recipes, because it looks like I'll be cooking for Erik the Red tonight." Ms. Tremt laughs.

"Well, you'd better get started on that at home," I say, "before he does any more damage in here."

Ms. Tremt heads over to Erik the Red, takes his hand, and stares into his eyes. She definitely has an instantly calming effect on the Viking.

"One last thing," I call to her as she heads out of the library. "Whenever I forget where I put things, it's always because my mind is on something else . . . usually something I'm worried about. So if you can, try to get that thing out of your head for a while, and then you might be able to remember the last place you had your magical pen."

"I will try, Grace," Ms. Tremt says, waving good-bye. "I will certainly try."

CHAPTER	TITLE
2	Middle School Stuff

I'm so caught up in the craziness of finding a Viking in the library that it doesn't bother me as much as it should when I stumble out the main door of school. I hear a few kids snicker, but I decide that I'm going to be a better person and just ignore them—for now.

Hold your head high, I tell myself.

Unfortunately, holding my head high means that I don't see the skateboard that is lying on the ground at the entrance to the parking lot. I slip on it and fall into a swan dive, landing right on the hood of a car—Jessica's mom's car, of course. Jessica and Morgan are in the backseat, giggling, and I don't even want to think about what they're saying, so I just dash off in the other direction, even though it means that I have to walk an extra half a mile home.

My big sister, Bella, is making a smoothie in the kitchen when I get there. That's Bella's thing, these smoothie concoctions that sound like a perfectly horrible storm of ingredients but actually taste pretty good.

"Want to try some vanilla kale lime shake?" Bella asks.

"Not now," I say.

I didn't tell you that I cried a little on the way home, but I did. Maybe even more than a little. I mean, the Viking thing was pretty funny, but seeing your former friend laugh at you, and not for the first time, is a pretty sad thing. So yeah, my eyes may be somewhat red and puffy. A bit.

Bella notices. She pulls out a stool and gestures for me to take a seat at the counter. "You don't have to drink my shake," she says. "But you do have to tell me what's going on."

"Nothing," I say. "My allergies are acting up."

"Grace," Bella says in that big-sister voice that screams *I know you better than you think I do and you are not getting away that easily.*

"I'm just having a little social drama," I reply. "It's not a big deal. Just typical middle school stuff."

"Typical middle school stuff can be pretty brutal," Bella notes. "So spill."

"That's kind of the problem," I say.

"What is?" Bella asks.

"Spilling . . . and tripping . . . and dropping," I say. "You know, all the 'Graceless' stuff."

"Not that dumb nickname again," Bella says, shaking her head.

I know Bella remembers that day when I was in second grade. She played tea party with our dolls with me for hours that afternoon, even though she'd been over dolls for at least a year by then.

"Yup, that's the one," I reply.

"Forget them," Bella says. "They're not worth your time. You're smart, and talented, and beautiful, Grace. Who cares what a few mean kids say?"

19

"But what if one of the mean kids was some-one you thought was your friend?" I ask.

And then Bella puts her arm around me, and I start sobbing a little, because as you probably know, when you're trying to keep yourself together but have so many bad feelings inside, all it takes is one person to care—especially if that person is your mom, or your grandma, or your big sister—for it all to come rushing out like a tidal wave.

"It's horrible," I tell her. "And it's getting worse! They're laughing at me and talking about me all the time. I can feel it."

"Probably not *all of the time*, Grace," Bella says. "But even some of the time is rough."

"Can you tell me something, Bella?" I ask. "Why would someone who's been your friend for years, maybe not your *best* friend, but still your friend, and whom you've always been nice to, suddenly start acting mean to you?"

Bella squeezes her arms around me even more tightly.

"I don't know, Grace," Bella says. "Like I said, middle school stuff can be pretty brutal. Every-one's trying to figure out who they are and which crowd they fit in, and sometimes they think that to do that they have to step on other kids . . . even kids they've been friends with before. There are a lot of hurting kids in the halls of Sands Middle School. Believe me, I was one of them."

"That's not fair," I moan.

"It isn't," Bella agrees. "But the good thing about middle school is it's a pretty short period of time. And I can assure you, by high school everyone's pretty much figured out where they fit in, and they're a lot cooler about it."

"For real?" I ask.

"For real," Bella says. "I promise."

I decide to try some of Bella's green concoction, and it's actually pretty tasty, although it's a little salty with my dripping tears and all.

Bella grabs her bag and tosses it over her shoulder. "Speaking of high school, I'm going to the mall to meet some of my friends," Bella says. "Want to come and pretend you're in tenth grade too?"

Bella hardly ever asks me to hang out with her friends, so I'm a little tempted to say yes, but I think I'm going to pass.

"Thanks, Bella," I reply. "But I'm going to get

my homework out of the way and then get back to that book I'm reading."

"Is it good?" Bella asks.

"So good!" I say, finally able to smile. "I can't wait to finish it."

After Bella leaves, I fly through my homework and then reach under my bed to grab the book.

"Failure Is Not an Option." I laugh as I read the title aloud. "How could I forget that?"

The book was written by the NASA flight controller who led the Apollo 11 crew to the surface of the moon. It really is fascinating. I dive back into page 247 and lose myself in the space race. Jessica and Morgan . . . Ms. Tremt and Erik the Red . . . they all start to drift away as I soar toward the moon.

Failure is not *an option*, I think to myself when I put the book down later that night. I will not let middle school get to me. I'm in a great school. I have great teachers. I have great friends. If some kids aren't nice to me, well, then, that just says more about them than it does about me.

Now if only I believed it.

CHAPTER	TITLE
3	Some People

The next morning I wake up before my alarm clock even rings, take a three-minute shower, grab a cereal bar, and race out the door.

"Bye, Grace," my mom calls sleepily to me when she hears the front door open.

"Bye!" I call back. "Love you!"

I run-walk all the way to school without even worrying about tripping because I can't wait to see if see if Erik the Red is going to be sticking around Sands Middle School. When I open the door to the library, I can see that he is.

Eric's warrior armor has been replaced by a much-too-tight tracksuit, and it is the funniest thing I've seen in a long time.

"Do . . . not . . . laugh," Ms. Tremt warns me. "It took a lot of convincing to get him to wear this."

"I'm sure it did," I say. "You have incredible powers of persuasion, that's for sure!"

"I know," Ms. Tremt says proudly. "It is one of my skill sets."

"How about clearing your mind and figuring out where your pen is?" I ask. "Any luck with that skill?"

"That's actually been a little difficult with our Viking friend around," Ms. Tremt admits. "He is a rather fascinating fellow. Do you know his real name is Erik Thorvaldsson? Erik the Red was just a nickname he got because of his red hair."

"Were people making fun of him?" I gasp. "Look at him—they wouldn't dare!"

"I don't know about that, Grace," Ms. Tremt says. "But I do know that his family was exiled to Iceland when Erik was just a boy. That must have been tough, and painful."

"You know, I'm beginning to like him more and more," I say. "Maybe it wouldn't be so bad if he hung around here for a while."

Just then Erik sees a fly buzzing around the bookshelves and crushes it with a pounding fist.

"I'm not so sure about that," Ms. Tremt says. "He's a bit heavy-handed for middle school."

"True." I laugh.

"Would you mind keeping him busy for a few minutes?" Ms. Tremt asks. "Just until first period starts, of course. It's just been a little tough to think with all his banging and stomping. But I do know some good mind-clearing chants that might help me remember more about where I left that darn pen."

"No problem, Ms. Tremt," I say. "Come on, Mr. Thorvaldsson."

It's a little tough to say at first, but I know that nicknames can hurt, so I'm going to stick with Thorvaldsson, and not call him Erik the Red.

Ms. Tremt had hidden Erik's Viking gear in the secret room off of the library. I know, I forgot to tell you about that, but there's not much more to say other than to tell you that it's secret, and it's the place where all the time traveling begins.

I grab Erik's shield and spear and hold them out, asking him to show me some of his moves. He takes them from me and spins the spear around over his head effortlessly. Then he hands it back to me.

I grab the spear and lift it over my head, but it's a lot harder than I expect it to be. I try to twirl it around and decide that I definitely need two hands to do that. Unfortunately, I start to twirl it in the direction of Erik's head, but the spear lands in a bookcase. I try to pull it out, but I can't budge it. Erik grunts, pulls it out, and hands it back to me.

Then he crouches down onto the floor, sweeping his spear around my feet so fast I have to jump over it or be knocked down. Can you guess which one? Yup, I got knocked down.

Erik lets out a bellowing laugh that fills the library. Our substitute teachers have been a little weird in the past, but it was going to be pretty tough to pull this one off. Even in the tracksuit, he seems like he comes from another place and time. (Which he does!)

"Aha!" Ms. Tremt shouts from her previously quiet corner of the library.

She scuttles across the room and grabs a metal water bottle off of her desk. Then she opens it and tips it over. Her magical pen spills out onto the desk.

"Um . . . that's kind of a strange place to put a pen," I observe.

"Exactly!" Ms. Tremt says. "And the last place *some people* would look!"

"Are we talking about *some people* specifically, or in general?" I wonder aloud.

"Specifically," Ms. Tremt tells me. "But not specifics that I can get into detail about now. Let's just say that when Erik showed up, I had a feeling that he wasn't alone."

"Got it," I say. "I'm glad you found your pen, and I hope Mr. Thorvaldsson has a nice trip home, but I've got to run to class now."

And as if I had set the clock myself, the bell for first period rings just then.

"Please come see me later, Grace," Ms. Tremt

calls after me. "There's something I'd like to run by you, if you have the time."

"I always have time for you, Ms. Tremt," I call back as I run toward math class.

I would like to tell you that the rest of the day went as smoothly as the morning in the library went. It started off pretty well. Sure I dropped my pencil a couple of times in math class and nearly fell out of my seat reaching for it, but I didn't. And yes, I heard a few giggles and snarky comments when I dropped the ladle into the soup pot and the cafeteria lady had to fish it out for me, but I was able to rise above them.

Until gym class.

It's my least favorite class of the day, as you can imagine. I know it's going to be even worse than usual when I see Jessica, Morgan, and their friends gathered around the volleyball net, tossing a ball back and forth.

"Hey, Grace," Morgan calls over to me.

I look around the gym, just in case there happens to be a new girl also named Grace in school. It doesn't look like there is. It looks like Morgan is calling to me. Maybe even in a kind of friendly manner.

"Hey, Morgan," I call back, trying to be cool about it and not appear too eager or overly friendly.

"What'd you get on your social studies test?" Morgan asks when I walk over to her.

Huh? I'm pretty confused, but maybe my plan is working. Maybe when I just ignore the giggles and the snark, they realize I'm a lot cooler than they think I am. Maybe Morgan remembers that she actually liked me once upon a time and that I'm still the same person I was back then.

"Oh, I got a ninety-seven," I say proudly. I had studied really hard for that test.

"Ugh. Show-off." Jessica snickers at me.

The other girls nod in agreement, as if I had just said I thought I was the greatest thing since the first moonwalk.

"Totally Graceless," Morgan agrees.

What is going on? I thought Morgan really wanted to know what I got on the test. Was it some kind of trick? Did I do something wrong? Because I really didn't think there was anything wrong with answering her question, but obviously it was some kind of huge error.

I'm mortified. I want to just run out of the gym and never step foot in Sands Middle School again. I head over to Ms. Casey, our gym teacher, and tell her that I'm feeling queasy.

"Queasy? Like 'I need to go to the nurse' queasy?" Ms. Casey asks.

"I think I'll just head to the bathroom first, if that's okay," I say. "And if I don't feel better, I'll go to the nurse."

"Okay, Grace," Ms. Casey says. "Here's a hall pass. Just tell the nurse to call me if you decide to go to her office."

I slip down the hall and into the bathroom, and then I sink into a stall. I'm getting tired of all these tears, but I can't help myself. I don't understand what just happened. It doesn't make any sense. Why would Jessica and Morgan go out of their way to be mean to me?

I know that the longer I stay in here, the harder it will be to go back and face them again, so I decide to think about Bella's words. Middle school doesn't last that long. If I can just get through days like this, I'll be fine.

I shuffle toward the gym, but I'm moving as slowly as I possibly can, when I hear someone calling my name.

It's Ms. Tremt.

"Did you get hurt in gym?" Ms. Tremt asks, concerned when she sees my puffy eyes.

"Just my feelings," I admit.

"That can be equally painful," Ms. Tremt says. "Are you sure you're ready to go back there?"

"I don't know," I say. "I thought it would be better if I did."

"Sometimes it's better to take some time for yourself," Ms. Tremt advises. "Why don't you go to the library? It's empty right now, and I can tell Ms. Casey that you're going to rest there until you feel better. She'll understand."

"But you won't let . . . ?" I start to say.

"I won't let the other kids hear," Ms. Tremt says. "Don't worry."

I sigh with relief. I would have gone back to the gym, but I definitely feel better about spending some time by myself right now.

Except that I don't get to spend much time by

myself, because Ms. Tremt sits down across from me two minutes after I take a seat in the library.

She looks deeply into my eyes again, but this time she looks a little . . . I'm not exactly sure . . . a little angry maybe?

"Grace, I need you to tell me what's going on," she says. "And I need you to be truthful."

I explain to Ms. Tremt everything I told Bella the day before and add the story about what just happened in the gym on top of it.

"I wasn't showing off. I really wasn't," I tell her. "Morgan just asked me what I got on the test, and I told her."

"Grace, it was a setup," Ms. Tremt says. "I know it's hard, but sometimes people don't care about hurting your feelings. Sometimes they even go out of their way to hurt them."

"Why?" I ask.

"I don't know, Grace," Ms. Tremt says honestly. "But I do know that no one is going to be able to make it better except for you."

"But I didn't do anything wrong!" I protest.

"I know," Ms. Tremt says. "Neither did I, but do you think I don't know what some of the kids say about me, Grace? Do you think it doesn't hurt my feelings?"

"I didn't think it bothered you at all," I admit. "I mean, they don't even know how cool you are—time travel and all. If they did, I'm sure they'd all want to be hanging out with you in the library all the time."

"Exactly," Ms. Tremt says. "And they don't even know how cool you are."

"Well, I thought Morgan did . . . ," I say sadly.

"Then obviously she forgot," Ms. Tremt says. "But I know, and Matt knows, and Luis knows . . . and if you spend your time focusing on the people who don't know, you're going to forget how cool you are too.

"This might be something that you'll never figure out," Ms. Tremt continues. "And I know that's hard, because you like figuring things out, and I'd like to know why they've decided to be mean to you too. The important thing is to remember that there are always going to be things that make you feel bad, but you can make those feelings smaller if you surround yourself with happy things."

Of course, right then two happy things appear in the windows of the library doors—Matt and Luis.

"We heard you weren't feeling well at gym," Matt says. "Can we help?"

"Is it 'girl trouble'?" Luis jokes. "As in girls named Jessica and Morgan?"

"Something like that." I laugh.

"I'd like to help put those girls in their place," Matt says. "Who do they think they are?"

"Thanks, guys," I say. "But it will probably just make things worse. I'm okay, really. I just have to rise above it."

"Well, if you need me to lift you up, you know where to find me," Luis says.

"At the skate park?" I ask.

"Yes, and you should definitely come there with me after school today," Luis says. "Matt's coming too."

"Oh, I'd like to, but I told Ms. Tremt I'd stop by later," I say.

Ms. Tremt waves her hand. "Another time, Grace. You should take the rest of the day to have fun with your friends . . . your real friends.

Tomorrow's fine. We have plenty of time," she says with a wink.

I believe her. Because if anyone has plenty of time, it's definitely Ms. Tremt.

CHAPTER	TITLE
4	Blown Away

I could stay at the skate park all afternoon, watching Luis spin his board and grind on the rails, but there's a book in my backpack that is calling my name, and after an hour I decide to tell Matt and Luis that I need to go. They can tell that I'm in a much better mood, because I really am, so they tell me they'll text me later and then they get back to the tricks and flips.

The sun is still shining brightly, so I walk to the other side of the park and plop on a bench. I love to read, anyplace, anytime, but I love reading outside on a sunny day more than anything.

I reach into my backpack and feel the thick pages of *Failure Is Not an Option* in my fingers. I turn to page 286 and dive in. I don't even notice that while I'm obsessed with reading, someone comes and sits on the bench next to me until a familiar voice startles me. "I *love* that book."

It's Jay Kapoor, my friend from fifth grade. We worked on our science fair project together that year, and of course we won, but we don't have classes together anymore, so I haven't seen him in a while.

"I couldn't stop reading it," Jay says. "I was totally obsessed. I'm not sure I even ate until I was finished with it."

"Me too." I laugh. "Until now, because you made me stop."

"I'm so sorry," Jay says. "That was really rude of me."

I give Jay a friendly shove on the shoulder and smile. "I'm kidding," I say. "I only have a couple of chapters to go." I smile and shut the book.

"Don't let me stop you!" Jay protests. "Seriously. I don't mind waiting. I've been dying to talk to someone who's read the book too. And I can finish my math homework while you read."

"It's a deal," I say, flipping the book open again.

Jay's pencil moves quickly and silently across his math workbook while I read. I let out a big sigh when I finish the last sentence. I hate that feeling when you're so absorbed in a book that you can't wait to get to the end, but then when you do get to the end, you know that it's over and you're going to miss being inside of it.

"So . . . ?" Jay asks.

"So I'm blown away," I reply. "I loved learning about all the nuts and bolts of the mission— literally!"

"Me too!" Jay says. "It's like he explained every little operational detail! I felt like I could control a mission myself after I read it."

"Imagine if we could!" I say dreamily. "Imagine if we could have been some of the first people to look at the Earth from the moon. When we look the other way all the time!"

"Or even to be in the control room!" Jay says. "Having a hand in making history!"

We both sigh, lean back on the bench, and take a minute to imagine it. There really aren't any words when you're geeking out so hard. And we are.

Our dreams are interrupted by Jay's digital watch alarm.

"I've got to get to robot club," Jay explains.

"No worries," I say. "I should get home myself."

"We should talk more, though," Jay says as he waves good-bye. "About the book, I mean."

"We should," I agree. "Text me later if you want."

"Sounds like a plan," Jay says. "Get home safe!"

Bella's busy making another smoothie when I get home, but this one is bright pink with some gelatinous balls in it. I don't care how good it tastes. I am not touching that one.

"Better day?" Bella asks.

"Actually, worse," I admit.

"Really?" Bella says. "Because you look a lot better than yesterday."

I tell the story—again—about what happened during gym class.

"Ugh, I just can't with those girls," Bella says. "What's their problem?"

"I don't know," I say. "But I'm going to rise above it."

"That's a perfect plan," Bella agrees.

I tell Bella about my time in the library with Ms. Tremt—the advice time, not the Erik the Red time—and my afternoon in the skate park with Michael and Luis and then later on the bench with Jay.

"I'm trying to focus on the happy things," I explain. "So that even though there are things that make me sad, they won't matter as much. And I'm going to grow a thick skin and not let the mean girls get to me as much."

Bella ruffles my hair. "But not too thick." She laughs. "I kind of like my emotional little sister. It makes me feel like I'm not alone."

I jump up and hug Bella. "You're not," I say. "Ever."

My skin feels pretty thick the next day at school. At least thick enough to get me past a few clumsy mishaps and the snarky comments that follow them. I can see that Matt and Luis are on high alert, and it makes me laugh. Even though we have different schedules, every time something happens, like when I let my thumb get in the way of the water fountain and it made the stream of water fly down the hall, they suddenly appeared by my side, like they were daring anyone to come between us.

I also wasn't bothered as much because I had something important on my mind. I had spent the evening texting with Jay about the book, and then I started thinking about traveling in space, and then my mind wandered to time traveling, and that's when it hit me—Ms. Tremt had something to run by me, if I had time. If I had time to time travel! I'm sure that's what she meant!

I rush into the library as soon as last period ends and look around to make sure no one else is in the room. "I believe you want to send me on a mission," I announce to Ms. Tremt. "And I know exactly where I'd like to go."

Ms. Tremt doesn't look as excited by the idea as I thought she would, though.

"I'm afraid that's not a possibility at the moment, Grace," she explains. "I do need you to go on a time-travel journey for me. But I'm afraid this trip will be different. I'm sorry, but I'm going to have to choose the time and the place for you. The world depends on it."

I shake my head disbelievingly. Am I hearing Ms. Tremt correctly? Matt got to choose where he took us. I wouldn't have picked Brooklyn in 1951, but I understood why he did. He wanted to make sure his grandfather avoided an accident and became a Major League Baseball player. And he did!

I'm trying to focus on happy things. I really am. I spent the whole night focusing on space travel, and time travel, and the chance that I might get to be part of the mission that traveled to the moon for the first time in human history. And now Ms. Tremt has other plans for me? I feel just as crushed as I did in the gym yesterday. Maybe middle school just isn't meant to be a happy time in my life after all.

CHAPTER	TITLE
5	Spaced Out!

I thought Ms. Tremt would be sensitive to my feelings and maybe even reconsider if the fate of the world actually did depend on the mission she had planned for me. I mean, there are 567 other kids at Sands Middle School. Maybe one of them could take this trip for her and I could get the time-travel vacation of my choice. I decide to propose that option to her, since she doesn't seem to be thinking about that on her own.

"Ms. Tremt, I really appreciate that you think so highly of me you would give me this crucial mission," I say, trying to sound very appreciative. "But maybe there's someone else you could choose for this one? There are lots of other kids in the school."

"Oh no, Grace," Ms. Tremt says. "None who are as suited for this mission as you are."

Ugh! This isn't going the way I want it to go.

"Thank you, Ms. Tremt," I say, trying again. "It's just that, well, I kind of had my heart set on going somewhere that's special to me."

"That's lovely, Grace," Ms. Tremt says. "I'm sure you will find this mission special as well."

Then Ms. Tremt leans in and whispers in my ear, "I can appreciate how hard you're trying, Grace, but I'm not changing my mind about this. Sorry."

"It's okay." I sigh. "I'm sorry. I should have known you wouldn't ask me to do it if it weren't important."

"Correct," Ms. Tremt says. "And now I need you to help me with something."

Ms. Tremt leads me toward a bookshelf, then reaches in between two books and pulls out some small pieces of wire.

"Hold on to these, please," she says, handing the wire to me. "And follow."

We head toward another shelf, and she pulls a sheet of gold foil from the top. "Don't fold it," she warns. "Next . . ."

Next is a small metal wrench that is shoved into the side of a file cabinet. After that is a ring-shaped piece of plastic, some more wires, and a few pieces of paper with some complicated diagrams drawn on them.

"I think that's it," Ms. Tremt says.

"That's what?" I wonder.

"That's what you'll need to bring on the mission," Ms. Tremt explains. "You see, Grace, Houston has a problem."

I'm puzzled, and I'm usually pretty good at putting puzzle pieces together, but they're not fitting just yet.

"I don't think I understand," I admit. "What are all these things, anyway?"

"It's serious, Grace," Ms. Tremt says, and suddenly she looks very serious, like, *Girl, it's about to go down* serious. And that makes me nervous.

"There has been some time-travel tampering

lately," Ms. Tremt explains. "As I mentioned, I am asking you to travel through time not for your own pleasure, or to make your own small change. I am asking you to travel through time because the fate of the world depends on it."

Have I mentioned my heart is racing right now? It's beating as fast as it was that time I let Matt and Luis talk me into going with them to see the new zombie movie, the one with the tagline that said, "You won't be dead for long."

"That sounds really exciting, Ms. Tremt," I say, this time not even thinking about how much I want to walk on the moon but worried that there may actually be a kid better suited for this mission than I am. "But like I said, maybe there's someone else you want to ask? Because it's not like I'm very athletic . . . or even coordinated, really. You know that people call me Graceless, right? There's a reason for that. What if I mess up? Because I do, all day, every day."

"I do not need an athlete," Ms. Tremt informs me. "I need someone supersmart, with a good and true heart. And that's you."

"Gee, thanks," I say nervously. "But can you

tell me a little more about this mission first? I mean, just to be sure I can handle it?"

"I'm afraid I can't," Ms. Tremt says. "There are people—and dark forces—working against me. Recently they have been able to tamper with a most important historical event, and if the tampering is not fixed, the history of the world will change with drastic aftereffects. I need someone with a stellar brain, a master logician. Again, this is why you're perfect for the task."

Heart pounding . . . even faster.

"Well, just because I got a ninety-seven on a social studies test doesn't mean I'm all that," I say humbly.

"I know," Ms. Tremt says. "But you are 'all that' and *more*, Grace."

Ms. Tremt explains a little more about the mission, without going into too much detail.

"Do you remember that in your trip back with Matt, his mission was to make one small change?" Ms. Tremt asks.

"How could I forget?" I laugh. "One small change that didn't affect other areas—like who Matt's grandfather would marry."

"Exactly," Ms. Tremt says. "So now think about the repercussions of one change in a major historical moment. For example, consider if George Washington had decided not to cross the Delaware River on Christmas, 1776."

"I'm thinking," I say. "His soldiers would definitely have been warmer."

"True," Ms. Tremt says. "A small change. But also one with huge repercussions. Because then what if the Battle of Trenton never happened, and the revolutionaries were defeated by the British instead of the other way around?"

"Then I'd guess we'd have taxation without representation," I say. "And maybe we'd be drinking a lot more tea?"

Ms. Tremt laughs. "A *lot* more."

"So I'm heading to 1776," I wonder, trying to prepare myself for the mission, whatever it may be. I'm not looking forward to it, though.

"Of course not." Ms. Tremt laughs.

She holds up the wires and the plastic ring. "Do these look like things that George Washington would have needed?" she asks.

"Um, probably not?" I guess.

"Definitely not, Grace," Ms. Tremt says matter-of-factly. "Plastic was not invented until 1907."

"Oh, right," I say. "How could I have forgotten about that?"

"You are headed to a much more modern era," Ms. Tremt says dramatically. "One that pushed the frontiers of the future in ways that had never been seen before."

"YOU'RE KILLING ME, MS. TREMT!" I yell. "TELL ME NOW!"

"Compose yourself, Grace," Ms. Tremt says. "You are heading to 1969. These items have been taken from the Apollo 11 spacecraft by an enemy of mine who is trying to change major events in history. If you don't replace them, the American astronauts' first flight to the moon might not take off. Are you interested, Grace?"

I've never fainted before in my life, but I feel myself getting light-headed when I hear Ms. Tremt's words. She quickly grabs a chair and places it under me.

"Ms. Tremt!" I gasp. "Are you serious? Did you know?"

"Did I know what?" she replies.

"Did you know that the Apollo 11 mission is exactly where I wanted to time travel to?" I cry.

"Now, how would I have known that?" Ms. Tremt asks with a wink.

I smile and then take a deep breath. "Could you excuse me for a minute?" I ask Ms. Tremt.

"Do you need me to leave the room?" Ms. Tremt asks.

"No, but if you could turn around, that would be great," I say.

Ms. Tremt looks puzzled, but she turns around and faces the bookshelf. I jump up from the chair, pump my fists, wiggle my hips, and do the goofiest happy dance you've ever seen.

"All done," I say when I'm finished. "I just have one more question."

"What is it?" Ms. Tremt wonders.

"Can I bring some friends along?" I ask. "The way Matt got to bring Luis and me?"

"You may," Ms. Tremt says. "But only one friend for this trip, unfortunately."

"I only need one," I tell Ms. Tremt excitedly. "And I know just the right one!"

* * *

I am so going to blow Jay Kapoor's mind—when I find him. I dash through the hallways, looking from locker bay to locker bay, but I don't see his dark, wavy hair that sweeps perfectly over his left eye anywhere.

I decide to check around the outside of the school, just in case he's decided to stop and chat with someone about, oh, I don't know . . . robots, or spaceships, or time travel, perhaps. I am grinning ear to ear just thinking about it when I accidentally bump into a girl who's bent over tying her sneakers. Of course, when the girl looks up, it turns out to be Morgan, but when she sees me she quickly looks away. No giggles, no snark, just nothing. She's alone, so maybe she doesn't have to prove herself by making fun of me. I don't even care, though, because I am in a happy place—a very, very happy place.

I wander past the park, just in case Jay happens to be sitting on a bench doing some math homework, but he's not there, either. On the way home, I text Jay to see if he might want to stop by my house after dinner.

. . . to talk space travel, of course. ☺

Cool! I'll be there!

Mom and Dad know Jay from our science-fair-project days, so of course when I tell them before dinner that night, they are totally down with the plan.

"Hey, Jay," Dad says when he answers the doorbell. "You guys working on a new project?"

"We are!" I gush. "But Jay doesn't really know about it yet. So if you'll excuse us . . . we need the dining room table."

"It's all yours," Mom says. "After you and Bella finish putting the dishes in the dishwasher, of course."

I slump my shoulders. Parents, can they ever cut you any slack?

"I've got it, Grace," Bella calls, being a big-sister lifesaver again. "Go get to work."

I plop *Failure Is Not an Option* on the dining room table and sit across from Jay.

"Are we really working on a project?" Jay says. "Science fair happened months ago. Do you already want to start on one for next year?"

"Nope," I answer. "It's not a science fair project. It's not exactly a project, really. It's more like a mission." I try to keep calm, but my heart is pounding.

"Like an Apollo 11 mission?" Jay laughs.

"That's not as much of a joke as you think it is," I say mysteriously. "But yeah, something like that. Are you in?"

"I'm in," Jay says. "So what do we need to do to get started?"

"We won't actually get started until tomorrow," I explain. "Can you meet me in the library after school?"

"I can," Jay says. "But you could have just asked me that in a text. Why did you want me to come over?"

I pull out a notepad and two pencils and put them on the table next to the book.

"Because we need to know the details of this mission as well as Neil Armstrong," I say. "So let's take some notes."

CHAPTER	TITLE
6	An Open Book

When Jay shows up at the library the next afternoon, it's clear he's taken my suggestion to a whole new level. He's got a pile of books so high in his arms that he can barely see over them, and from the titles on the spines I can tell that they're all about the Apollo 11 mission.

"You did realize that you were coming to a *library*?" I say. "There are plenty of books here. You didn't have to bring your own."

Jay laughs. "These were just sitting on my bookshelf collecting dust," he says. "I figured if you were serious about knowing every detail, I might as well bring them along."

I grab the top book off the pile and invite Jay to come tell me all about it. The thing is, I need to distract him for a minute . . . or maybe more . . . because right now Ms. Tremt's in the secret room dealing with a new unexpected library visitor, Trieu Thi Trinh. (I had never heard of her before, but according to Ms. Tremt, she was a total hard-core Vietnamese warrior from the third century.)

I leave Jay at the table for a minute and peek in on Ms. Tremt, who is pressed with her back up against the wall while Trieu shows off her masterful swordsmanship.

"You haven't noticed an elephant around, have you?" Ms. Tremt asks worriedly.

"Why, did you lose one?" I laugh.

"Not funny, Grace," Ms. Tremt says. "Trieu Thi Trinh usually rode an elephant into battle, and I'm not quite sure how we'll explain that one if it ends up in the library somehow."

"Nope, no elephants," I reply. "Did you lose your pen again?"

"I have it right—" Ms. Tremt says, then stops.

She pats her pockets, then takes off her shoes and looks in them one at a time. Finally, she takes off her scarf and shakes it out. The magical pen goes flying across the room, and Trieu bats it out of the air with one of her swords.

"Impressive," I say. "But how about we send her home and show Jay how this 'mission' is going to work."

"Good idea," Ms. Tremt says.

I go get Jay and bring him into the secret room.

"Wow. How did I never notice this was here?" Jay asks as he looks around. "Is this a new addition?"

"Hardly," Ms. Tremt replies. "You'd be surprised at the things people miss that are right in front of their eyes."

I cough a few times, just to cue Ms. Tremt that there is a Vietnamese warrior standing on the other side of the room.

"Is she part of the mission?" Jay wonders, noticing Trieu.

"She is not," Ms. Tremt says. "But she is going to help me demonstrate some of the logistics of it."

"Okay. I can't wait to see this," Jay replies.

"Good," Ms. Tremt says. "But first I must warn you, Jay, this mission requires a serious time commitment."

I notice Jay looking down at his watch and I get nervous. I don't want robot club to get in the way of this.

"But it won't interfere with your other stuff," I assure him.

"I must also warn you that this particular mission does involve some risk," Ms. Tremt says to Jay.

"Cool," Jay says. "Sounds like fun."

I look down at the floor. I know Jay has no idea that Ms. Tremt is talking about real, serious risk. And I kind of don't want him to think too much about it either.

Ms. Tremt takes out *The Book of Memories*. I can see that Jay's impressed by its shimmering metallic cover.

"I haven't read that one before," he says.

"I know." Ms. Tremt smiles.

"It's a classic," I say with a grin.

Ms. Tremt holds the book out to Jay so he can

open the front cover. He sees the words printed on the opening page in gold leaf.

To sign out this book requires special permission. Please see librarian Valerie Tremt.

"It's a good thing you're here," Jay says. "Is signing out the book part of the mission?"

"It is," Ms. Tremt replies. "But first someone else needs to sign it out."

Ms. Tremt uses her magical pen to sign her name on the card, and the book begins to sparkle with a green glowing light, swirling around the page until Jay and I read the question it forms aloud.

"'Where would you like to go today?'"

Jay rubs his eyes and looks at me. "Are we working on some kind of magical chemistry mission?" he asks. "Because that's pretty cool if it is!"

"No, it's not chemistry," I reply. "But it is pretty magical."

Ms. Tremt writes *Vietnam, 238 CE*, with her pen and nods, satisfied.

Then she places the book against the wall and tells the two of us to stand back.

The book grows higher and wider, and its

pages stretch out until they fill the wall of the secret room like a projection screen.

"Please open the book now, Jay," Ms. Tremt instructs him.

"Grace," Jay whispers to me. "What is this?"

I smile at him. "Open the book, Jay," I say. "I promise, you're going to love this."

Jay opens the book, and a battle scene appears on the wall. Huge, in the center of the scene, is Trieu Thi Trinh's elephant. The Vietnamese warrior yelps and rushes over. Before we can even say good-bye, she jumps onto the back of her precious pachyderm and it runs away.

"What the what?" Jay says disbelievingly. "What did I just see? Nope, no way I just saw what I think I just saw."

"You saw it," I reply. "It's Ms. Tremt's secret specialty. Time travel."

"It's the truth," Ms. Tremt explains. "That is indeed my specialty. Grace has been part of a mission already, but she cannot reveal the details of it, just as you may not reveal the details of the mission that you are about to embark on to anyone, ever. If you choose to accept the mission, of course."

"He's going to accept it," I say. "Trust me."

"Do I get to decide?" Jay says. "I mean, Ms. Tremt did say there's risk involved. I'm really not a very risk-taking kind of guy. I thought she was exaggerating."

"He does have a point, Grace," Ms. Tremt says. "Honestly, I hate that I have to ask you. If I could do this mission myself, I would. Unfortunately, that is both incredibly dangerous and an impossibility at this time."

"Of course it's Jay's decision," I say. "I'm going with or without him. But I'd rather go together."

"Then can somebody please tell me what this mission is?" Jay asks.

Ms. Tremt hands me the collection of items that need to be returned to the spacecraft.

"Do these look familiar?" I ask Jay.

"Not particularly," Jay says. "Are they from some kind of maker kit?"

"They are from Apollo 11," Ms. Tremt explains. "And if they aren't brought back to 1969 and put in the right position before the next launch, history will be changed forever."

"But what *are* they?" Jay says.

"I'm not quite sure, but I am sure you'll figure it out once you're in the spacecraft," Ms. Tremt says as calmly as if she were giving us the weather report.

"We have to go. The world is depending on us," I tell Jay.

"Indeed it is," Ms. Tremt echoes.

"So what you're telling me is, Grace and I are going to step inside that book and walk into the year 1969," Jay says.

"Yes, that is what I'm telling you," Ms. Tremt agrees. "Kennedy Space Center, Florida, in 1969, to be exact."

"Well, what are we waiting for?" Jay shouts. "Let's go! The world is depending on us!"

We do have to wait for Ms. Tremt to review the time-travel rules with Jay. They haven't changed— no bringing anything from the future into the past, like cell phones or money dated past 1969. We have to wear clothes that are appropriate for the time, and we get to carry these really awesome scarves that can be used in case of emergency.

"But only in case of emergency," Ms. Tremt explains. "They're still in beta mode."

"Hmm," Jay says. "Still some glitches?"

"There may be," Ms. Tremt says. "But in a pinch, if you wrap the scarf around yourself, you will appear to be dressed in appropriate clothing . . . at least for a few minutes. You will also be able to understand and be understood in any languages that happen to be spoken."

"I guess that could come in handy," Jay says.

"It has," Ms. Tremt replies.

"Of course, some of the regular time-travel rules will have to be bent for this particular mission, because of its gravity," Ms. Tremt adds.

"'Gravity' meaning 'seriousness,'" I say. "Because it's just a myth that there's no gravity in space."

"Correct," Ms. Tremt replies. "You don't have to worry, though. I know people in high time-travel positions. I can assure that while rules can be bent, none will broken."

We're not really worried. We're too busy thinking about the spacecraft . . . and the moon . . . and the astronauts . . . and WE ARE GOING TO NASA!!!

Ms. Tremt pulls out some clothes for us, and they're not really that bad, although I don't think

Jay and I would care if we had to wear clown suits as long as we were going to Apollo 11.

Jay gets a pair of faded jeans shorts, a striped T-shirt, and a pair of Chuck Taylor All Star sneakers. I get a groovy green jumper and sandals. It is July in Texas in 1969, so we need to look—and feel—cool.

Ms. Tremt also hands us a pair of NASA visitor badges and a couple of walkie-talkies.

"Yes! We can say our parents work at NASA and we're visiting them!" I cheer.

"That's the idea," Ms. Tremt says with a nod.

"And that they gave us walkie-talkies so we can keep in touch with them," Jay says. "But can we take these?"

Jay holds out the folded pages of the Apollo 11 notes we made the night before.

"Sure," Ms. Tremt says. "But don't let anyone else see them. It would be odd for you to know the level of detail for a mission that hasn't happened yet. Now, one last thing."

Ms. Tremt takes the wires, the wrench, and all the other things we'd gathered from the library and puts them into a cardboard box.

Then she wraps it carefully with packing tape.

"You'll have to carry this with you," she tells us. "And figure out how to get all the pieces back in place before the ship launches."

"How in the world are we going to do that?" I start to worry.

"Remember why I chose you, Grace," Ms. Tremt reminds me. "Heart . . . brains . . . You'll figure it out."

Jay and I look at each other and then at Ms. Tremt. Mission accepted, and we are ready to roll.

Ms. Tremt hands me her magical pen, and I use it to write on the card.

Kennedy Space Center, Houston, July 16, 1969, 8:30 a.m.

"Grace, what are you doing?" Jay asks, alarmed. "The Apollo 11 spacecraft takes off from Titusville, Florida! Houston is the command center."

"Oh shoot!" I gasp, scribbling out Houston and writing *Titusville* over it.

"You'll have an hour before launch to get everything fixed," Ms. Tremt tells us.

"And then two hours after that to explore?" I ask.

Jay looks at me curiously.

"We get a three-hour time-travel window," I explain.

"This trip will be a little more flexible time-wise," Ms. Tremt says. "You will have as much time as you need. But try to get back as soon as you can. There are some who would be happy if my mission failed, and I'd like you to be as far away from them as quickly as you can."

She puts the card in place and opens the book. The Apollo 11 spacecraft appears before us. I am so filled with energy and excitement that I can barely contain myself. I grab the box and start to step into the scene with Jay, and everything is just about as perfect as it is ever going to be, until I trip and bump into Jay, and the picture starts glitching out and I can see it flip back and forth between Florida and Houston, then Florida again, then Houston, and . . .

CHAPTER	TITLE
7	July 16, 1969. 8:30 a.m. (1 hour, 2 minutes until blastoff)

So here I am, inside of Apollo 11, and Jay is nowhere to be seen. I know I'm in Florida, because that's where the Apollo 11 spacecraft is, but Jay, well, who knows? Also, the box with our precious cargo is busted open, and the pieces that were inside are now scattered everywhere.

"I knew she chose the wrong person," I moan. "The biggest mission of my life—maybe of life on Earth—and here comes Graceless!"

I start to crawl around to pick up the pieces, but there's not actually that much room. It's easy to see the wrench, so I grab it first and toss it in the box, and then I grab some of the wires and the plastic ring.

So if you've seen the pictures of the Apollo 11 spacecraft, you might be confused about the lack of space. I mean, at 363 feet tall, it does look like a tall building. The thing is, most of what you're seeing is the engines and fuel tanks that make up the different rocket stages.

On top of all that is the lunar module, which is what the astronauts will eventually use to get to the surface of the moon. During the trip to space, though, the legs of the lunar module are folded up, and it's just sitting under the command/service module, waiting for its turn.

That's where I am now—the command/service module. It will house the astronauts for the trip to the moon and back, and almost all of their equipment as well. The command module is about the size of a minivan inside, and that's a lot smaller than I'd imagined it to be. It's amazing to think that three grown men are going to eat, sleep, and work in here for five days. I take out the notes Jay and I wrote for the trip and flip to a diagram we made, but it's pretty simplistic and not very helpful.

Suddenly, I hear a low whisper coming over the walkie-talkie.

"Grace? Jay to Grace," says the whisper.

He's here! Well, not here, as in, together with me in the command capsule, but at least here in 1969.

"Hello?" I whisper back. "Klutz here."

I can hear Jay breaking up, and I focus on listening to the words he's saying.

"Grace . . . are . . . you . . . okay?" Jay asks through a lot of static.

"I'm fine," I say. "Where are you?"

I can't hear Jay's response, but I know there's no time to panic. He's alive, and okay, and I have an important mission to focus on right now. We'll figure out the rest of it later.

My mission: Figure out where all these random things belong. It shouldn't be difficult, because there's not that much room in here. I spy a tool kit and figure that I should probably check it out. It's a good thing I do, too, because there's an empty spot where a tool clearly should be. I take the wrench I brought from the library out of the box and check to see if it fits into the spot in the kit. It does!

Then I head over to the control panel and start to search for the different places where wires might belong. I wrap the wires around the loose ends to put them back in place too. While I'm crawling around that side of the module, I find a case where the diagrams fit perfectly. That just leaves the plastic ring and the gold foil.

"Waste," I hear Jay say over the walkie-talkie.

"What?" I yell back into it. "Jay, where are you?"

No response.

Then I hear Jay again. "Waste-management system," he calls through the buzzing sounds of static.

"Gross," I complain to myself. But I figure I'd better go check it out.

I crawl around the module and find the waste-control panel underneath the vacuum cleaner stowage. Vacuum cleaners on a spacecraft—who knew?

Then I see what Jay's talking about. There's a tube in the waste-management system that is missing a ring. I screw the plastic ring in place and make sure it's really tight. Now I just have the foil left.

"Jay!" I whisper-yell into the walkie-talkie. "I need you! The foil!"

"Grace?" Jay says, confused. "Is that you?"

"FOIL!!!" I yell. "JAY! FOIL!!!"

"Foil?" Jay asks.

"YES!" I shout. "FOIL!!!"

I'm not sure what Jay says next, but it sounds something like "Lunar module."

Is he kidding me? I have to get the foil to the lunar module? I don't know how I'm going to pull that off, but I'm going to have to, I guess. The whole world depending on me, and all.

I open the hatch of the command module, then make my way down to the lunar module. I search desperately to see exactly where that particular piece of foil needs to go. . . . Have I mentioned that I'm pretty good at solving puzzles? The answer is not coming to me just yet, though. And that's when I hear banging and clanging noises, followed by laughter and friendly banter.

I've heard the sound of those voices before, watching old NASA videos on my computer.

They're coming from Neil Armstrong, Buzz Aldrin, and Michael Collins, the three Apollo 11 astronauts. And they're getting closer.

"JAY!" I call desperately into the walkie-talkie. "Where are you? I need to get out of here—now!"

I hear Jay's voice faintly, but it sounds like "*Gzzpfzzrdeeglpp.*"

It's panic time. My mind runs through all the different scenarios that could get me out of this situation.

First scenario: I could walk out of the lunar module and start my search for Jay on the ground.

There are a couple of big problems with this scenario, the first being that I have no idea where Jay is or how I will find him. Plus I still have to get the foil in place. Also, if the astronauts—and anyone really—see me now, they'll think I tampered with the mission, and this trip will probably never launch. It could drastically change history.

Second scenario: I use *The Book of Memories* to go back home. But I have no idea where Jay is, so if I leave, I'm leaving without him, and that's not an option. I don't know if we'd ever be able to find him again. And if I don't get the foil back in place, no mission accomplished.

It looks like I'm going to have to go with scenario three: Join the astronauts on their mission to the moon and figure out where to put the foil—if I can stop myself from hyperventilating first, of course.

I try one last time.

"JAY!!!" I cry into the walkie-talkie. "WHERE ARE YOU???"

"*GZZPFZZRDEEGLPP*" is all I get back.

"Failure is not an option," I remind myself.

"I'm going in, Jay," I tell the walkie-talkie, hoping somehow Jay can hear me even though I can't hear him. "And you better stick around until I get back."

I cross my fingers and start to crawl inside the lunar module. As I'm crawling, I can see a bare patch where the foil needs to be placed. I get to work, hoping that my pounding heartbeats aren't as loud as the clanging I'm hearing all around me right now.

I'm not sure it's going to be possible to survive the journey to the moon in here, but it doesn't look like I have any other options at the moment. I'm just hoping that somehow, someway, Ms. Tremt and her time-traveling team have got my back.

"GRACE!" Jay calls frantically over the walkie-talkie. "The astronauts are making their way to the command module!"

Duh! I already know that, Jay. Unfortunately, every time I reply to him, it seems like he can't hear me. I have no clue what to do next.

I wish there were another way. I really do.

I'm open to suggestions, people. Do you have any good ones?

CHAPTER	TITLE
8	
	8:50 a.m. (42 minutes until blastoff)

I peek outside the lunar module's windows. The astronauts are standing outside, arm in arm, posing for pictures. An army of reporters shouts out to them and photographers push one another out of the way, trying to get the best shot.

I remember seeing a backup space suit and some rations in a storage pod right under the hatch of the command module. I know the astronauts will be climbing in any minute, so I'm going to have to grab them as quickly as I can. Graceless needs to stay far away from me right now.

I slip back through the lunar module hatch as quietly as I can, fumble around the command module hatch, and then find the storage pod. I quickly grab a suit and some food pouches.

You probably already know that the food is dehydrated, right? You have to mix it with water, but even then it still looks like the least appetizing thing on this planet—or any other. They are vacuum-sealed in plastic packages. The package labeled PEAS looks incredibly similar to the stuff I've seen in my baby cousin's diapers. Yuck. Hopefully, it tastes better than it looks. There are even some thermo-stabilized hot dogs and packs of brownie bites.

"I may even gain a pound or two up here." I laugh to myself, looking at the brownie bites and climbing into the space suit.

Suddenly that thought leads me to another anxiety-inducing one. The Apollo 11 is already carrying 6.2 million pounds of spaceship. The engineers have carefully calculated the takeoff and trajectory of the entire trip based on very precise measurements. What if my extra ninety-five pounds changes the whole mission?

My heart starts doing that pounding thing as well. Ms. Tremt's words echo through my head. *A good and true heart. A stellar brain and master logician.* She believes that I am all of those things. She believes in me.

I sit back and close my eyes. The voice of Ms. Tremt that is ringing in my head starts to sound more like my mom. I remember the words that she always tells me whenever I have a problem.

"The smartest people don't know all the answers, Grace," my mom says. "The smartest people know that they don't have all the answers and that they need help finding them. And they know the right people to ask for help."

I take out *The Book of Memories.*

"I've got this, Mom," I say.

Then I cross my fingers and try to believe that my words are true.

CHAPTER	TITLE
9	9:05 a.m. (27 minutes until blastoff)

I need a Brainiac Dream Team to help me, and I also need to stop the clock from ticking down to launch time. It's a good thing I have a magical book in my hands.

You need to know the right people to ask for help, I think. *This is a complex math and science puzzle. So the right people will be the best math and science thinkers.*

If I can use *The Book of Memories* to travel in time and bring back some people who can help me figure out my problem, I'm pretty sure that after I return them, I'll come right back to this moment, so no time will have passed. I can still take the trip to the moon and figure out how to find Jay when I get back.

I think about everything I've learned in school and read in my favorite books. I set my mind on Ms. Tremt, and the library, and then I think about one of the greatest libraries in all of history, in the great Egyptian city of Alexandria. The city was founded by the leader Alexander the Great in 332 BCE and was a center of learning in the ancient world.

Those ancient philosophers were able to figure out really tough problems all on their own, without any computers or other technology, I think to myself. *I could use one of them.*

A dreamlike vision of a woman appears in my head, her hair wrapped up in a messy bun and wearing scholar's robes.

"Hypatia!" I cry. "Of course!"

Hypatia was a Greek mathematician and philosopher who lived and taught in Alexandria. She learned math and astronomy from her father and was the first woman that we know of to make an important contribution in the field of mathematics. She taught her students how to design an astrolabe, a portable astronomical calculator. She sounds perfect, right? I think so too!

I frantically write *The Library at Alexandria, 380 CE,* and somehow the scene appears before me even though there's even less room inside the lunar module than in the command module. Somehow, magically, *The Book of Memories* scene appears life-size, even though the space in here is jam-packed.

I cross my fingers, wrap the beta version of the scarf around myself, and hope that when I step inside I will actually find Hypatia at the library and that the magical scarf will work. Imagine if today's a day she decides to check out a play or something? And what will happen if I show up in Alexandria wearing a space suit?

The time-traveling fates are with me, though, and I see a large group of students surrounding Hypatia in the main room. No one seems particularly disturbed by my presence, so thank you, magical scarf beta version.

"Excuse me, pardon me, student coming through," I mumble as I push my way through the crowd of students, trying not to knock any-one down.

Amazingly, my clumsiness seems to be an advantage here, because as I stumble my way through, students begin to step aside so I don't actually elbow them or step on their toes.

I must look really desperate, because when I finally get to Hypatia and grab her hand, she follows me without asking a word.

"I need your help," I tell her as I pull her into a room. "I have a complex problem that I need to solve. It's urgent, and the next few minutes are going to seem pretty crazy, but I promise you'll be back here in no time, and it will all seem like some weird dream."

"The oracle never mentioned anything about you," Hypatia says. "But I never met a problem I didn't want to solve, so let's go!"

That's my math girl! I don't think Hypatia became the woman that she is without taking a lot of risks, so she seems totally on board with the plan, even after I write the Apollo 11 coordinates on *The Book of Memories* card.

Remember, it's really a tight squeeze in this

capsule, so I'm closer to Hypatia than I ever imagined I'd be, and let's just say that I'm glad the people of ancient Egypt were known for their fragrant perfumes.

"I'll be right back," I tell Hypatia. "But here's the problem I need to work on. Imagine that I can fly to the moon in this thing. But it was designed to carry 6.2 million pounds, not including my ninety-five-pound body. So I need to know: Will my weight affect the mission? And if it does, is there anything I can do to make it work?"

"The moon!" Hypatia says dreamily. "Does Selene know about that?"

"Who?" I wonder.

"Selene, the goddess of the moon, obviously," Hypatia replies.

"Oh, right, she's totally down with it," I answer. "I got her approval at the temple, of course."

"Lucky girl," Hypatia says. "I've always wanted to explore the universe!"

"I'm sure, Hypatia, but unfortunately, that's not in the plans for you today," I say. "This is a 'solve the problem' moment only. As you can see, there's not even really room for me in here."

"Okay, but I have a question for you," Hypatia says. "Do you know what holds the moon up in space?"

"Um . . . gravity?" I reply.

"No." Hypatia laughs. "Moonbeams!"

I laugh out loud and then leave Hypatia to think about the problem while I figure out who else I can grab from the pages of history to help. And yes, it is already a tight squeeze in here, but we're talking "the world depends on you" kind of stuff, so I think we can all suck it up for a few and add another member to the team, right?

I decide that member should be a physics expert, but now I have a dilemma. Sir Isaac Newton or Albert Einstein? They're pretty much one and two on every "top physicist of all time" list. I don't even know how a girl's supposed to make that choice. That's like needing to write a pop song and trying to choose between Beyoncé and Taylor Swift. Could you do it?

It turns out, I can't choose, so I'm not going to. Why should I, anyway? The more the merrier, and if that power trio can't figure out my problem, I might as well stay in ancient

Alexandria for the rest of my life.

Next stop: Newton's family farm in Woolsthorpe, England, 1666.

Are you wondering why I'm not heading to Cambridge, where Newton studied and later taught? It's because the Great Plague is ripping through Europe, and the university is closed until further notice. Plus I know it will be easier to find him when he's living at home. Smaller space and all.

There's not really any polite way to interrupt someone who is working on developing his foundational theories of light and color, so I go for a direct approach. Sir Isaac Newton is so deep in thought anyway that he doesn't even notice I've popped into his room.

"Hey, Isaac, I need your brain," I tell him.

"Pardon?" he asks, puzzled.

"I need you to take a quick trip with me," I explain. "Just to help me with a complex puzzle. Then you can get back to your theories."

"It might be a needed diversion," he admits. "I'm having a difficult time deciding whether to divide the color spectrum among six or seven colors."

"Tricky," I say, figuring it's better to keep it to myself that I think his eventual choice of seven was the wrong decision, based on the infinite colors of the spectrum and stuff like that.

A quick scribble and we're back in the lunar module. Hypatia's still giggling about her moonbeam joke. It's like I never even left!

"Hypatia of Alexandria, meet Isaac Newton," I introduce them. "Isaac, this is Hypatia. Hypatia, this is Isaac."

"Hello, Isaac, it's nice to meet you," Hypatia says. "Do you know what satellite is full of cows?"

"Do tell," Sir Isaac Newton says.

"The mooooon." Hypatia laughs. Isaac cracks up too.

"I'm writing a book about antigravity," he tells Hypatia.

"Really?" she asks.

"Yes, and it's impossible to put down!" he jokes.

"Very funny," I say. "But remember, problem solving 101. That's why you're here. I'll be right back."

I'm racking my brain trying to think of the best place to track down Albert Einstein. I could go to

Princeton University, where he was a professor of theoretical physics in the 1940s, but it's a pretty big campus, and I'm a little tired of running around.

I could also go to Israel after World War II. Einstein helped establish the Hebrew University of Jerusalem, and he was even offered the presidency of the State of Israel, but he turned it down.

I'm feeling the need to have a small target, though, so I'm going to head to the patent office in Berne, Switzerland, in 1906, where Einstein was a technical assistant. It's pretty mind-blowing to think that a genius like that was working at a government job that didn't require a whole lot of thinking, but when I get there, I can easily see why it would work.

Young Albert Einstein is the life of the patent party. Everyone in the office seems to like him, and he jokes with all the people who come in and out. He's going to fit right in with Hypatia and Sir Isaac Newton!

I know it's going to be a challenge to get him away from his desk, though. I've read that Einstein managed his time precisely: exactly eight hours of patent office work, eight hours of miscellaneous and scientific work, and eight hours of sleep. (Except that he wasn't such a great sleeper; sometimes he would be awake for days, and he often used his sleep hours for writing.)

"Al, can I interrupt your work?" I ask. "It's important."

"I'm not really supposed to leave my desk," he replies.

"Not even for a bathroom break?" I ask.

Albert Einstein laughs, and it's kind of infectious, so I start to giggle too. I think that convinces him.

"Just to be clear, you're not actually going to the bathroom, but I promise that you will not be away from your desk longer than a bathroom break takes," I explain.

"I'm intrigued," Einstein says.

"You have no idea!" I laugh.

It is nearly impossible for the four of us to fit inside the lunar module. It's like squeezing into the clown car you see at the circus. I'm getting afraid that it's actually going to be impossible for anyone to think in here. Luckily, in addition to having great minds, Hypatia, Sir Isaac Newton, and Albert Einstein all seem to be pretty cool and go-with-the-flow. Or at least, so wrapped up in making each other laugh that they're going with the flow at the moment. Which works for me.

What doesn't seem to be working, however, is the group's focus. They're so busy telling jokes that they're not really paying attention to my problem!

"I was up all night wondering where the sun had gone," Einstein says. "Then it dawned on me . . ."

Hypatia and Sir Isaac Newton clutch their sides as they howl with laughter.

"You're killing me," Isaac says.

"FOCUS!" I yell sternly. "We've got a problem to solve. There's no time for jokes!"

So if I had a few more decades of math class under my belt, I might be able to tell you all about the details of their calculations, but quite honestly, I'm not sure I'd even be able to write it all down, which I can't anyway at the moment. Let's just say it involves a lot of big numbers and words like "gravity assist" and "spacecraft trajectory" and "acceleration rate" and the one word that I definitely do not want to hear—"crash."

"At launch, the spacecraft will have to travel about 1.5 feet per second, and it will continue to accelerate to speeds of 4.6 miles per second," Einstein calculates. "The first stage of rocket engines will have to burn through 203,000 gallons of kerosene and 318,000 gallons of liquid oxygen before separating from the spacecraft and falling back to Earth. Then the second stage will ignite and burn through 260,000 gallons of liquid hydrogen and 80,000 gallons of liquid oxygen before it, too, separates from the spacecraft and falls back to Earth."

"Okay," I say. "What does that mean?"

"It means that about one thousand gallons of fuel will be burned every second," Hypatia explains. "So your ninety-five pounds will not make a significant difference to the spacecraft's trajectory."

"Well, that's a relief," I say.

"There is something to consider," Sir Isaac Newton interrupts. "Even though your weight is statistically inconsequential to these calculations, your movements inside the module could have a small effect on the spacecraft's orientation, and even its trajectory."

"Therefore, no jumping jacks in space," Einstein adds.

"Dude, there is hardly room for a push-up in here," I tell him. "You don't have to worry about that."

I'm ready to clear this module. I thank Hypatia, Sir Isaac Newton, and Albert Einstein for the use of their brains, and their jokes, and then use *The Book of Memories* to return them to their respective time periods and places. I keep my fingers crossed that the time-travel authorities will somehow figure out a way to erase their minds, or make them think this all was actually a weird dream, so there aren't horrible repercussions in the fabric of time or anything. I'm kind of hoping that's what Ms. Tremt meant when she said that the people she knows in high time-travel positions could bend the rules a bit.

The lunar module feels a whole lot roomier when I return there alone. It's 9:30 a.m., only two minutes to go before launch. I can hear the astronauts busy in the command module above me.

I go over a checklist of things I need to do to prepare for launch. Most importantly, I make sure I'm correctly connected to the module's oxygen tubes. I know that at some point I'm going to have to meet the astronauts because the lunar module won't be coming back to Earth, so I'll have to join them in the command module. But at least the mission will be unstoppable then.

I'll just have to convince the Apollo 11 astronauts that I'm some kind of group space hallucination or something. Easy-peasy.

At 9:31 I get myself set because I know as soon as the engines go off, it's going to become a loud and wild ride, but I listen to the sound of static over the walkie-talkie. It relaxes me, though I'm not sure why. I just focus on it and hope that Jay knows I'm okay. And then, for a few seconds, I hear him.

"Be safe, Grace. I believe in you," Jay whispers. "Wow, it's getting really rumbly in here."

"In here, too," I whisper back to him. I don't know if he hears me.

"T minus fifteen seconds. Guidance is internal," I hear a commanding voice say. "Twelve, eleven, ten, nine . . . Ignition sequence start . . . Six, five, four, three, two, one, zero . . . All engines running . . ."

CHAPTER	TITLE
10	9:32 a.m. Blastoff

"LIFTOFF!" the Mission Control voice cheers. "We have a liftoff, thirty-two minutes past the hour, liftoff on Apollo 11! Tower clear."

I hear Neil Armstrong reporting from the command module, and I know that I am in safe hands. These three astronauts have spent their whole careers preparing for this moment, and the team of people on the ground is equally dedicated to the mission.

The rumbling gets even rumblier as we climb up into the sky, and my cheeks feel like they are going to detach from my face. After what seems like an eternity but is probably more like ten minutes, the ride starts to get a lot smoother.

I can't see anything outside, even though there's a window in here, because the lunar module is surrounded by protective panels right now. I'm glad I read that book, because I have a really good idea of what's going to happen next. If I didn't, I'd be sitting in here all alone and totally freaking out. I'm kind of freaking out a little as it is, but I'm going over all the steps of the mission in my head, and that is helping.

Here I am, sitting in the lunar module, coasting toward the moon, and well . . . to be honest, guys, I think I just dozed off for a little bit. I do that on car rides all the time; it's kind of my thing. It's funny if you think about it—I defy Sir Isaac Newton's first law of motion. When my body is in motion, it tends to rest. (Okay, sorry for that, I think Hypatia's jokes are getting to me!)

I know that pretty soon the astronauts are going to have to separate the command module from the third stage of Apollo 11's rocket. Then they'll have to turn the command module around and attach it to the lunar module. I'll be able to see, finally, because the protective panels will come off. But for a few moments I'll be alone out here in the lunar module, not attached to anything. If something goes wrong, that's how I'll stay. It's pretty scary.

But I have total confidence in the guys. Even though we haven't met yet, I feel like I know them because I've read so much about them. Buzz Aldrin has already served as a fighter pilot in the Korean War and flew in sixty-six combat missions. Neil Armstrong served as a navy aviator in the Korean War too. Another navy pilot, Michael Collins, was part of the Gemini 10 mission which was NASA's sixteenth manned flight. He walked in space just three years ago. I think they've got this covered.

I can feel the impact when they fire the explosive bolts that cause the main spaceship to separate from the rocket. They blow apart the protective panels on the lunar module. I'm not going to lie, my heart is racing and I can feel panic flow through my body. If things go wrong, I'm toast, totally stranded out in space. On the positive side, now I can see!

Guys, the view, it's unbelievable. From here, outer space looks like sparkly diamonds sprinkled on black velvet. And looking at the moon from here? You know how the moon looks like a giant glowing beach ball with some dark patches when you see it full on a really clear night? Well, now I can tell that it really is a giant sphere of rock. I can see the cavernous craters, and the monstrous mountains. They're breathtaking.

"It's a view worth the price of the trip," as Neil Armstrong will later say. And somewhat scary, too, although no one says that.

I hold my breath as they turn the ship around and reconnect with the lunar module—and with me! I'm safe! Whew! That only took about three and a half hours from takeoff.

Now I have time—a lot of it—to spend with myself. We left on Wednesday, and we won't land on the moon until Monday! I spend hours and hours checking out every single spot of the lunar module, every button, every wire, and comparing it to the notes I made. I draw some diagrams, too. I'm not great at technical drawing, but really, there's nothing else to do.

I have some long imaginary conversations where I say the things I wish I could say in real life. I tell Jessica that I think she's one of the meanest people I've ever met, and I can't understand why she's so mean to me. I tell Morgan how much it hurts that she would be part of the group that's always making fun of me, especially since we used to be friends. I'm glad that no one's around to watch me, because they would definitely wonder what is wrong with me, but it's good to get everything off my chest, even if it's only to myself.

When I get hungry, I eat some of the astronaut food. The peas taste almost as bad as they look, but the brownie bites are kind of yummy. Then again, I'm starving, so crumbly chocolate-flavored powder works for me at the moment.

I also sleep, a *lot*. I guess I didn't realize how tired I was, but once you're in a coasting spaceship and you're staring out into the vastness of space, the drowsiness just pretty much overtakes you.

I'm actually glad I sleep so much, because it's really lonely in here, and I'm starting to miss my friends, and my mom and dad, and Bella. There are times when I feel like I just can't do it, it's just so lonely and the thought of spending any more time in here makes me want to open *The Book of Memories* and go home. But then I think of Jay, and the chance to actually go to the moon, and I suck it up.

Finally, after hours and hours and days and days, I know when I hear and feel the main engine fire up, and the spaceship slow down, that we're getting close to moon-landing time.

First we need to be captured by lunar gravity and pulled into an orbit. Then I hear some banging and clanging overhead, and I know that my time alone is about to end.

The hatch opens, and Neil Armstrong and Buzz Aldrin crawl into the lunar module. I don't have to tell you, they aren't expecting to find me in there. They've been in battle, they've been through the most grueling training, they've learned how to stay calm in the face of death, but I can tell that seeing me nearly puts them over the edge.

Luckily, I've had plenty of time to prepare my story.

"Hey, guys," I greet them. "I know that you

must be feeling pretty shocked to see me right now. So let me tell you, you're not actually seeing me. I'm not here. I'm not real. It's a kind of space science magic that I can't really explain but does exist."

Michael Collins stayed back in the command module, and I hear him calling to Buzz and Neil over their radios. Both astronauts check in to let him know they're okay, then quickly cut the radio transmission off.

"Kind of space magic?" Buzz Aldrin says gruffly.

"Okay, maybe not magic," I say. "Would you believe, some weird group hallucination?"

"That would be more believable," Neil Armstrong says.

"Let's go with that, then," I say cheerfully. "The fact is, you're going to think I'm here with you. And I'm not really. But you have a mission that needs to be completed. I know you've trained a long time for it. I know you want to make history. So here's my question to you: Are you going to let something like a silly hallucination of a girl in the lunar module, which you know can't possibly be real, get in the way of your mission? Or are you just going to move ahead as planned?"

"Move ahead as planned," Buzz says seriously. He's a mission-first kind of guy.

"I thought so." I smile. "So even though I'm not really here, let me introduce myself. I'm Grace, and I'm incredibly happy to meet you."

"Hi Grace," Neil says. "I don't think I'm actually happy to meet you, at least not out here in space, but welcome to the *Eagle*."

"Thank you," I say.

Then I nod my head at Buzz, because I don't think he's really ready for social formalities at the moment.

"You should get to work," I tell them. "Just pretend I'm not even here. Because—again—I'm not, really."

Buzz is happy to take my advice. They tune back in to the radio transmission, and Michael Collins reports that the landing craft is heading down to the lunar surface.

"Everything's going just swimmingly," Collins says. "Beautiful!"

Neil Armstrong slows the engine and prepares for the tricky landing. When he sees that we are about to hit a crater that is covered with large rocks, he steers the module to a smoother spot. I can practically hear our heartbeats pounding through the cabin. It's a tense moment.

As soon as the module's footpads touch down, Neil shuts off the engine.

Then he says into the radio, "The *Eagle* has landed."

That's the name of the lunar module, by the way. The *Eagle*. I think I forgot to mention that before.

Buzz reports on the view, describing what it looks like on the surface of the moon.

What can I say? It's a lot of rocks. I'm just kidding. It's actually really beautiful in a very unearthly way. Like a desert, but where everything's been painted a different hue of gray. Desolate, but absolutely stunning.

We're supposed to wait a few hours before heading out of the module, but Neil recommends that we start earlier than scheduled.

Buzz and Neil get all their gear ready and check to make sure everything is working properly.

"Don't mind me," I say, mimicking each one of their movements. "Just pretend I'm playing follow the leader."

All ready to make history, Neil opens the hatch and squeezes through the opening. He walks—actually slow-motion bounces—down a ten-foot ladder. He stops at the last step to make a report.

"I'm at the foot of the ladder," he says. "The LM footpads are only depressed in the surface about one or two inches. The surface appears to be very, very fine-grained as you get close to it. It's almost like a powder."

Then Neil Armstrong takes a step off the ladder, and it is the first time man has ever stepped on anything that isn't from Earth.

"That's one small step for a man, one giant leap for mankind," he radios.

Except that it isn't really a small step, it's more like a four-foot jump! When Neil steps away, I can see the very first footprint that was ever made on the moon. It's still there, you know. It should last about a million more years. That's because there's no wind or water on the moon, so no storms or other weather to wash away the footprint. It could possible get wiped out by a meteorite, though. The moon gets bombarded with space rocks all the time.

I turn to see Buzz holding up a camera, taking pictures from inside the lunar module. He actually turns and grins at me. I feel like we're making some progress!

Buzz leans over and tells me that they were worried it would be difficult moving around on the surface, because of the reduced gravity and limited flexibility of the space suits. And because, well, no one has ever done it before! It doesn't look like Neil's having any trouble.

"It's my turn," Buzz says, as he takes his camera and crawls through the hatch too.

Buzz lowers his camera down to Neil, then climbs down the ladder. Now it's Neil's turn to take pictures of the second man to walk on the moon.

I know they have three experiments to complete on the moon. They start the first one and drive a pole into the dusty rocks. Aluminum foil hangs from the pole, and it will be used to hopefully collect particles of solar wind that can be brought back to Earth and analyzed.

Then, in a picture-perfect moment, the astronauts take a United States flag and press it into the surface of the moon.

I'm grinning from ear to ear as I watch all of this, because I know exactly what's going to happen next. The president is going to call the astronauts and tell them that this has to be the proudest day of all of our lives as Americans. It is.

I'm surprised by what happens after that. I know Neil and Buzz are supposed to set up the second experiment, but instead Neil turns the television camera away and waves to me.

"Me?" I gesture, pointing to myself.

Buzz points back to me, as if to say, *You!*

Wow. I did not expect this. I didn't actually expect that I'd really even get here. Jay and I obviously didn't plan this all out very well, and I was totally content to just have joined the astronauts on this epic journey. But to actually get a chance to walk on the moon? Just wow.

So what are you waiting for? Let's go!

Before I open the hatch, I think about all the thousands of steps it took to get to this place. All the plotting and planning, all the engineering and building, all the training and missions, and all the hopes and dreams of so many people who have been wanting to explore a brave new world for so very long. And here I am, little old Grace, all because of Ms. Tremt and her magical book. Don't worry, I know how incredibly lucky I am.

I climb down the ladder, and it's a very strange feeling when I finally step into the moondust. I'm not exactly weightless, but I can move a lot easier. The moon has one-sixth the gravity of Earth, so I'm not even sixteen pounds here! But I'm not floating, either. I'm just super light on my toes, at least as light as you can be wearing a heavy space suit. It's a little like being on a giant trampoline.

I wave to Neil and Buzz, then take a few giant leaps over to them. I can leap like the most amazing ballerina! My moves are totally made of awesomeness. It's pretty easy to glide across the surface too, although Neil and Buzz have to show me how to stop by digging my heels into the moondust.

Neil holds up the camera and snaps some pictures of me as I dance across the surface of the moon. I never imagined I could feel so graceful wearing this enormous outfit, but I do. I glide some more, then twirl and leap in front of the camera.

I'm really glad Neil and Buzz are here with me, though, because I know I would get really scared, really quickly, without them. It is lonely, very lonely, on the moon. There is gray dust and rocks that sparkle, there are some hills and craters, there is a jet-black sky, and there is us. And only us.

I know I can't take any more time out here—Neil and Buzz have work to do, and the whole world needs to watch them. So I climb back up the ladder and crawl into the hatch. When I take my helmet off I can smell the moondust that has collected on me. It sort of has a burnt ash smell, the way our town park does after the Fourth of July fireworks celebration every year.

I head back in and watch the astronauts complete their experiments and take some more photos. Then Buzz and Neil crawl back into the lunar module. Mission Control tells us to go to sleep, since it will be a while till we can reconnect with Michael Collins back in the command module.

Speaking of Michael Collins, this is what Mission Control said about him orbiting the moon while we were down on the surface:

"Not since Adam has any human known such solitude as Mike Collins is experiencing during this forty-seven minutes of each lunar revolution when he's behind the moon with no one to talk to except his tape recorder aboard *Columbia*."

Later, when the command module has almost completed its orbit around the moon and is coming back to get us, the astronauts start to pack up everything they've brought with them and also gathered: soil samples, film, and rocks. They have to leave a lot of things behind, but they take one very special souvenir back with them. It's a piece of fabric and wood from the Wright Brothers' first flyer, the first successful powered aircraft, that Neil put in the lunar module. From the first flight to the first flight to the moon!

This is when the trip gets scary. While they're packing, Buzz notices something lying on the floor of the lunar module. It turns out to be a circuit breaker switch that had somehow gotten broken off. (It wasn't me—I swear!)

It's not even a switch to a vacuum cleaner, or a waste system, either. It belongs to the breaker that will activate the engine that will lift us off the moon so we can get back to the *Columbia,* the command module. So if the circuit isn't switched, we're not going anywhere.

Buzz asks Mission Control for help, and they tell the astronauts to get some sleep while they figure out the problem. Yeah, right, like any of us are going to be able to sleep right now!

I hear Buzz and Neil talking it over. Because it involves electricity, it is too dangerous to try to flip the circuit with a fingertip, or anything metal, and most everything small enough to work in here is metal.

And that's when I have an Einsteinian inspiration! I'm jotting down some notes on my diagrams when I look at the tip of my pen. It's felt! Not metal.

"Buzz!" I say excitedly. "Will this work?"

"Let's give a try, kiddo," he says.

Buzz pushes my pen into the opening that the switch fell out of. He pushes it in, and amazingly, it works! We're going home! Hooray!

"I'm glad you're here, even though you're not." Buzz laughs.

"Me too!" I reply.

Everything in place, we lift off and reconnect with *Columbia*, then head back into the command module. It takes some convincing to assure Michael Collins that he's just part of a group hallucination, but eventually he buys into the story. There's not much left to do now but sleep, and that's just what Neil, Buzz, and Michael do.

CHAPTER	TITLE
11	Homeward Bound

While those three are sleeping, though, my head starts to hurt. I realize that Jay and I were so focused on helping Ms. Tremt with her problem, or as she would say, "the world's problem" that we kind of boxed ourselves into a corner in our rush to get the Apollo 11 mission off without a hitch.

Don't get me wrong. I'm proud that we are a part—a big part—of making sure the astronauts made it to the moon. And I'm grateful—really grateful—that I made it there too. But as I sit here, it suddenly all becomes clear to me. I rushed. I rushed to get the pieces back in place, I rushed to find out if I could stow away on the flight, and I rushed to make my final decision about whether or not I should stay on the flight.

What I didn't consider is that in the end, if I stick with this mission for the whole eight days it lasts, I am going to end up somewhere in the Pacific Ocean nearly one thousand miles away from Hawaii! There's not really going to be any place to hide or any way to explain that one to the news crews.

Also, I'm going to be far away from Jay, really far, and I'm not even sure exactly where he is. Hopefully he's in Florida, at the launch center. But I don't really know how my mistake—and my clumsiness—affected that glitch in the fabric of time. Jay may have gotten pushed into NASA's Mission Control in Houston instead. Worrying about Jay is making my head hurt.

As it is, either way Jay's already going to have to wait a seriously long time for me, making up excuses about why he's on a seemingly permanent field trip. Then, somehow, we're going to have to find each other. Have I mentioned that my head hurts?

There's got to be a better, smarter way to approach this. I try to channel the minds of the great thinkers I gathered from history. How would they tackle this problem? I'm not exactly sure, but I know they wouldn't give up.

"Is something wrong, kid?" Neil Armstrong asks while he dumps out some wastewater.

Astronaut. Not as glamorous a job as you would imagine.

"Maybe," I tell him. "But I don't think you can help. I need to meet up with a friend."

"That might take a little while, then." Buzz chuckles.

"Exactly," I say. "And I don't have a little while."

"Since you're not real and you have magical powers, can't you just pop out of here?" Michael asks. "Couldn't you just blink your eyes or wiggle your nose or do some other magic trick?"

"I could," I say, nodding my head. "That would be the plan. Except that I'm not exactly sure where my friend is. So I don't know where to pop to."

"I see," Michael says. "That is a problem. But maybe one we could help with? Don't let our flashy suits fool you—we're pretty smart guys."

"I know you are." I laugh. "But you've already got a lot on your hands."

"Not really," Neil chimes in. "Just a lot of wastewater, and I could use a break from that."

Without giving the astronauts too much detail about exactly where Jay and I are from, or how we got here, or why I need to get back to him, I give them the basics. Jay is somewhere at NASA, but I'm not sure exactly where. We were talking on walkie-talkies, but then I lost him once the spacecraft left the atmosphere.

"The range of walkie-talkies is pretty limited," Buzz says. "So I'm thinking he's at the launch center in Florida."

"That's true," I admit. "But you know, there's also the possibility that those walkie-talkies could be . . ."

"Magical?" Buzz laughs.

"Maybe more like amplified," I answer. "I don't know a lot about their technology. The range could be bigger than we imagine."

"Did you hear anything in the background?" Michael asks. "It might be a clue."

"I did!" I say. "I heard a voice that counted down to liftoff!"

"So he could be in Houston at the control center," Neil notes.

"That's exactly the problem!" I wail. "He *could* be. I need to know for sure."

"Did your friend say anything else?" Buzz asks. "Think about it."

I try to think of Jay's last words, and thankfully they pop back into my head.

"Wow, it's getting really rumbly in here."

"He said it was getting rumbly!" I shout.

"FLORIDA!" Neil, Buzz, and Michael shout back. "He's definitely at the launch center. The rockets during liftoff make it feel like there's an earthquake in there."

It's so cramped that I feel like a group hug is going to really start invading everyone's very limited and precious personal space, so instead I simply hold my hand up and give each of the astronauts a high five.

"I'm sorry to say that I'm going to have to get

going now," I tell them. "And if you don't mind, it would be great if you could all turn away when I do. You know, secrets of magic and all. Even though I'm not really here."

The astronauts laugh.

"Sure thing, kiddo," Buzz says as he gives me a slap on the back.

"One more thing, guys," I say. "I know this is a little silly, but would you all give me a pinky promise that you're never going to tell anyone that I was in here?"

"I'll give you two of those," Neil says. "One for each pinky. We could never tell anyone anyway. Do you know how long the NASA psychologists would be grilling us if we told a story about you? We'd never get home!"

"Right," I say, nodding my head. "That would be a pretty unbelievable story."

We hold up our pinkies and twist them together, then pull.

"Pinky promise," Neil, Buzz, and Michael swear solemnly.

"Before you go, Grace, come over here for a minute," Michael says, leading me to the biggest window. "I think you have time for one last look."

I do. And it's so worth the time.

I see our planet, and it looks like a beautiful jewel, part sapphire, part emerald, part diamond. I can see the swirling clouds, the deep blue of the ocean, and the bright green patches of land. Everyone I know, and everything I love, is down there. Home.

It makes me think about a quote I read during my moon-mission-obsession period. It's from the astronaut Donald Williams.

"For those who have seen the Earth from space, and for the hundreds and perhaps thousands more who will, the experience most certainly changes your perspective. The things that we share in our world are far more valuable than those which divide us."

I stare at the image in the window and let it sink into my brain so I'll never forget it. Donald Williams is so right. I wish I could share this moment with all the kids at Sands Middle School. They might think twice about being mean to another person again. Seeing how small and fragile our world is just helps you see what really matters.

They say that Michael Collins is considered the forgotten astronaut because he stayed alone in the command module while Neil and Buzz made history walking on the moon. But I will never forget him.

"Thank you," I say to Michael. "It's been . . . magical."

Neil steps up to me, reaches his hand over to mine, and places something in it. It's a roll of film. I look up at him curiously.

"A little souvenir," he says. "Just promise you won't ever show it to anyone."

"Pinky promise," I say. "I won't."

Buzz, Neil, and Michael turn away from me. I take out *The Book of Memories*, hold it tightly so it doesn't float away, and write the information on the card: *Kennedy Space Center, Titusville, Florida, July 16, 1969, 10:00 a.m.*

I am pretty confident that it will be easy to find Jay in the crowd of people who had just observed the launch, but when I step into the scene, he's not part of that crowd. He is, however, not so hard to find, at least not after I stop and think like a robotics club member. I find him looking over diagrams with some of the NASA engineers.

Jay's face freezes when he sees me across the room, and he rushes over to me. "Did we fail?" he asks. "Please tell me we did not fail."

"We didn't," I say. "All systems go."

"That's a relief." He sighs. "So what are you doing here?"

I explain everything to Jay, and tell him how while we were being really smart in some ways, we were completely clueless in others.

While Jay and I search for an empty room where we can transport home, I fill him in on all the amazing details of my journey to the moon. Of course, he already knows the logistics of the trip, having read so many books on it, so I focus on the important stuff—what Buzz's favorite space food is (shrimp cocktail), what happens to moon rocks when you kick them, stuff like that.

"I wish you could have come!" I tell Jay.

Jay, though, is starry-eyed from his experience on the ground. He got to meet some incredible NASA engineers and learn all about their work and how they got started in their careers. He says it was the best ninety minutes of his life.

"I'd be happy if we could stay here for a week," Jay says.

"You almost did!" I laugh. "But I think it's time we get back to school."

We dip into a storage closet and set *The Book of Memories* for the Sands Middle School library. The scene that appears before us is not at all what we expect, though.

Oh, there are shelves and shelves of books, and tables, and laptops, and even Ms. Tremt, but she is being carried into another time portal by a strange man wearing green gloves. It's pretty obvious that she isn't thrilled about going on this trip, especially when we see her kick the guy in the shins.

"Ms. Tremt!" I cry. "We've got to save her!"

"There's two of us," Jay says. "And I used to go to karate class in third grade. I say we just step in."

"Great, Jay, but I don't think we can rely on your third-grade martial-arts skills," I say. "We need to rethink that plan."

"How about if we go in earlier?" Jay suggests. "Before the guy gets to Ms. Tremt."

"Now, *that's* a plan!" I say. "I'm just not sure if

it will work. The last time I traveled back in time, we just had our set mission within our time limit."

"Okay," Jay says. "But remember Ms. Tremt said this was a special mission. And that we could bend the rules of time travel a bit."

"She did say that," I agree. "It's worth a shot."

We change the card so we can get to the library fifteen minutes earlier, then step in. Ms. Tremt is excited to see us, but we hold our hands up to warn her that all is not right. We step silently into the library and tiptoe toward the secret room. Ms. Tremt follows.

"Is this because space is silent?" Ms. Tremt says. "Are you having trouble adjusting to life back on Earth, Grace?"

Hmmm . . . How did Ms. Tremt know that I went to space? That wasn't actually part of the plan.

"No, that's not it," I whisper. "We just saw some guy try to kidnap you from the library."

"Where is he?" Ms. Tremt asks, looking around.

I let her know that after we saw the kidnap scene, we went back fifteen minutes so we could warn her. Of course she agreed that it was an excellent plan but that we needed an even better one to foil him.

"Is he the guy who tried to mess with the Apollo 11 mission?" I ask.

"I believe he is," Ms. Tremt says. "Although I don't know if he is working alone or not."

"He looked alone when he was taking you through that other portal," Jay says. "So let's figure out what we're going to do in, oh, I don't know, the next ten minutes."

"I have an idea," I tell Jay and Ms. Tremt. "But we need a warrior—and an elephant."

"Trieu!" Ms. Tremt cheers. "An excellent choice of bodyguard, Grace."

We quickly work together to set the trap. We retrieve Trieu Thi Trinh once again. She doesn't look as confused as she was the last time she ended up in the library. Jay and I stay together with the battle queen in the secret room while Ms. Tremt goes back into the library.

"Tim," we hear her say to the bad guy. "Fancy meeting you in here. Although I can't say I'm happy to see you."

We hear them struggle—and then Ms. Tremt

tells him that she has something to show him.

"I have something that I think you want," Ms. Tremt says coyly.

"You have many things that I want," the bad guy, who I guess is named Tim, replies.

Jay and I whisper to Trieu, then get ready to open *The Book of Memories* again.

Oh yeah, you don't know the plan yet. Sorry!

We decided to get Trieu and tell her we had recruited a new warrior to fight with her. Then we would let Trieu take the bad guy back with her to third-century Vietnam. Trieu was definitely hard-core, so we figured it wasn't going to be so easy for Tim to get away from her.

So Ms. Tremt leads Tim into the secret room, and before we have to do anything, Trieu grabs him. She holds him tightly as she squeezes his biceps, I guess checking him out to see if he's going to be good on the battlefield. My early guess—not a chance. She does seem pretty interested in his long dark hair, though, and she starts running her fingers through it. So weird.

Trieu stares into Tim's eyes, then pulls him toward her and carries him into the battle scene.

"Buh-bye," I call to them, laughing.

"Now, that didn't at all go the way I expected it would." Ms. Tremt chuckles. "But it was very effective. Thank you, guys."

CHAPTER	TITLE
12	Mission Accomplished

Even though I'd love to know if Tim and Trieu end up living happily ever after, I have a feeling that the clock on that relationship is ticking down, and there are other things I need to check out.

I rush over to the nonfiction section of the library and grab a large, heavy book off the shelf. It's a book filled with pictures of the moon missions, and I flip through it to see if there are any photos of me, Neil, and Buzz on the moon. Nothing.

"Ms. Tremt, could I use one of the computers?" I ask.

"Sure, but don't forget to sign the log-in sheet," Ms. Tremt reminds me.

"Of course," I say, smiling. "I remember."

I sign the sheet and log in to one of the library's laptops. I enter "Apollo 11" into the search engine field and then click on the IMAGES tab. There are millions of entries but not a single one with me.

Ms. Tremt walks over and taps me on the shoulder. "We bent the rules, Grace," she says quietly. "But like I said in the beginning, we cannot break them. There is no record of your time on the mission, or of your space walk. That would most certainly be a rule-breaker."

I understand. I really do. I mean, who would ever be able to explain that one—a middle school kid from the future ends up as one of the first humans to walk on the moon with Neil Armstrong and Buzz Aldrin. But a photo of Graceful Grace would be pretty incredible. A girl can dream, no?

"You know, Grace, in this day and age,

everyone feels like they have to record each event with a picture," Ms. Tremt continues.

"That they post online." Jay laughs.

"Exactly," Ms. Tremt agrees. "But sometimes the best images are the ones we keep in our own heads and in our hearts. Our experiences are just that—ours. I believe you'll always be Graceful Grace, because you can keep that image with you forever."

I close my eyes and picture it. I can see me, tiptoeing through the powderlike dust of the moon's surface as gracefully as a ballerina. No one can ever take that scene away from me. Not even Jessica.

"Thank you, Ms. Tremt," I say. "As always, you are right."

"Not always." Ms. Tremt laughs. "But a lot."

Jay and I hug Ms. Tremt and thank her for giving us the experience of a lifetime. It's hard to leave the library after what we just saw, but homework—and robotics club—are calling.

Jay and I take the long way so we can walk past the park together.

"I have a proposal for you," he says.

"Let me guess," I reply. "A rocket project for next year's science fair? Or something with a space theme?"

"No," Jay says. "I want you to think about joining my robotics team."

"Me?" I ask, confused. "I don't know anything about robots!"

"You're a fast learner," Jay says. "I've seen you in action. And besides, we are totally a winning combination."

I go to punch Jay in the arm, but I trip over the top of his sneakers and we both fall into the water fountain. Jay pushes the button and we both crack up as we gulp up as much water as we can.

"Sure you still want me?" I ask, brushing some droplets off Jay's arm.

"I'm sure," Jay says. "I really think we could win! We make a great team."

Jay sends a stream of water right toward my face. "Let the war begin!" he cries.

We talk about robotics on the rest of the walk home. It's never been something I was interested before, but when Jay talked about the team, it sounded really cool. And I knew that even though I'd have to watch and learn for a while, once I found a couple of good books to help me figure it all out, I'd be able to contribute.

"You've almost convinced me," I say.

"Almost?" Jay wonders. "Why not all the way?"

I can't believe I'm actually going to tell Jay this, but we've just been through a pretty life-transforming experience, so I figure why not.

"I think I need to make some new friends," I tell him. "Friends who are girls."

"Perfect!" Jay says. "I'm so glad you just said that. My teammate is a girl, and I think you two would really get along."

"Really?" I say. "That would be incredible! Not that there's anything wrong with you . . . or Matt . . . or Luis . . ."

"I know." Jay laughs. "There are just some things we don't understand."

"Some?" I grin. "That's an understatement! But you've totally convinced me. Sign me up— Plus, it will be a good start to my new career goal," I tell Jay.

"What's that?" he asks.

"Being the first astronaut to walk on Mars!" I say. "What else?"

"Of course," Jay says. "And I'll be working as an engineer in the NASA control room, guiding your mission!"

Jay and I high-five each other. This is going to be fun!

Another afternoon, another smoothie. Bella is busy blending a midnight-blue drink that reminds me of the night sky. Sweet.

"You're looking unusually confident today," she notices.

I grin. Then I twirl around and curtsy to her.

"Wow, and graceful," Bella says.

I wish I could tell Matt and Luis about what just happened to me, because they'd totally understand the whole time-travel experience. I wish I could tell my mom and dad, because I know they'd be so proud of me. But most of all, I wish I could tell my sister, Bella, right here, right now. Because if anyone in the world would understand how much that mission meant to me, it's her.

Of course, I can't. So I switch to another topic that I know she'll understand too.

"I've decided not to let those kids bother me," I tell Bella. "Graceful . . . Graceless . . . I am who I am. If they don't like it, they're missing out."

"I couldn't have said it better myself," Bella agrees. "Except that, um, I think I did kind of say it better, a couple of days ago."

"Okay, I'll admit it, you were right, Bella," I say. "You told me so."

Bella sips her smoothie smugly, because really, those are the words all big sisters are just dying to hear.

"Oh, and one more thing," I say. "Do you know of any place where I can get film developed? You know, real old-school camera film? I sat in on the photography club today and took some pictures with an old camera we found in a closet. I'd love to see how the photos came out."

"If the film is black-and-white, I think my friend Declan can help you," Bella says. "He made his own darkroom in his garage and watched some videos on the Internet to learn about the process. He's actually pretty good at it."

"That would be great!" I say. "Maybe you could talk to him and figure out an afternoon when I could go over there."

"Sure thing, sis," Bella says. "I'd be happy to."

The rest of the week is pretty uneventful, but I mean, how could anything in the life of a typical middle school girl seem "eventful" after you've walked on the moon? I do get a photo-developing lesson from Declan and am able to somehow print my moon pictures on film paper. I come up with a story about how we have an assignment to re-create historical photos, and Declan buys into it hook, line, and sinker.

"You've got a real talent," he tells me. "You should think about going into photography. These really look a lot like those classic moon-landing photos."

"Thanks for the advice," I reply. "But I'm thinking more about becoming an astronaut, actually."

Declan is, of course, impressed, although I can tell he thinks it's probably never going to happen. I can't wait to prove him wrong.

Then, exactly one week after stomping on the

moon with Neil and Buzz, it's time for my next new life adventure—robotics club. I meet up with Jay after school and we take the bus together to the science center. The open space inside is filled with tables covered with pieces from robot kits: controllers, motors, cables, that kind of stuff.

Jay points across the room to a table in the far corner.

"That's our spot," he says. "And the girl with the ponytail—she's the one I was telling you about."

I can't get a good look because ponytail teammate is turned away from us, but when we finally get to the table and she turns around, my heart sinks. It's Morgan.

"Hey, Grace," Morgan says, not exactly making eye contact.

"Hey, Morgan," I say back, avoiding looking at her too.

Jay can tell something is up, but he's not giving up on his mission just yet. "So you two know each other?" he asks. "That's great!"

"You know, Jay, this may not have been such a good idea," I reply. "I'm really clumsy. I'll probably mess up the robot or something. Trust me, it will be a total disaster."

I start to walk away when Morgan taps me on the shoulder. "I know you're probably going to say no, but can we talk privately?" she asks.

I do want to say no, but I'm still trying to "rise above," so I agree to listen to what Morgan has to say.

"I know that saying sorry probably doesn't mean much right now," Morgan starts. "But, Grace, I've been wanting to tell you, I'm really sorry."

"For what?" I ask, trying to blow it off.

"For being mean," Morgan admits. "For believing that fitting in is more important than being nice."

"Isn't it?" I ask. "I mean, I get it. I'm an easy target. Graceless. I practically dumped that one into your laps. Who doesn't like to laugh at a good fall? It's sooo funny."

"You weren't the only target, Grace," Morgan says. "Trust me. And I'm so mad at myself."

"Why?" I ask.

"Because I let them talk me into not being

myself," Morgan says. "I was afraid they wouldn't like me."

"Well, if they didn't, it would have been their loss," I tell her.

"I get that now," Morgan says. "And that's why I'm sorry."

Morgan holds out her hand to me. As hurt as I am, I'm not going to be mean myself and make her suffer. I put my hand in hers so we can shake on it. And that's when Jay grabs us and pulls us into a big group hug.

"TEAMIES!" he cheers. "We've got a lot of work to do. Let's get going."

"Did you ever decide on whether we should use a wedge or a spinning blade design?" Morgan asks him.

"I don't know much about design," I tell them. "But there is one thing I want our robot to be able to do."

"What's that?" Morgan asks.

"Moonwalk!" I say.

Jay starts to moonwalk around our table, and Morgan and I join him. The other kids in the science center are all looking at us like we're crazy.

That's okay, though. They can laugh all they want. We know who we are—and we are winning this competition and bringing the trophy back to Sands Middle School for sure!

Failure is *not* an option.

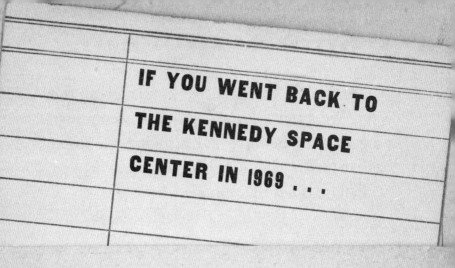

IF YOU WENT BACK TO THE KENNEDY SPACE CENTER IN 1969 . . .

You would find a lot of things similar to what Grace experienced. The command module was pretty cramped. It wasn't like the space shuttle, where there's room for the astronauts to move around freely. The food was packaged in plastic. It had to be rehydrated with water. The lunar module was connected to the command module until Neil Armstrong and Buzz Aldrin boarded it and landed on the moon.

The Apollo 11 mission was a historic event and fulfilled one of the goals President John F.

Kennedy had set forth for the United States in the early 1960s: to perform a lunar landing and return to Earth. Neil Armstrong, Buzz Aldrin, and Michael Collins were the astronauts chosen for the mission.

The returning to Earth wasn't a sure thing, though. No one, not the president, not the engineers at NASA, not Michael Collins who was orbiting in the command module, and not the other astronauts themselves, were sure that they were going to be able to get back to the command module once they landed on the moon.

In fact, there was a speech prepared just in case they couldn't. President Nixon would have said, "Fate has ordained that the men who went to the moon to explore in peace will stay on the moon to rest in peace. . . . For every human being who looks up at the moon in the nights to come will know that there is some corner of another world that is forever mankind."

Fortunately, the astronauts were able to reconnect with the command module and that speech never had to be given. They had Buzz Aldrin's felt-tip pen to thank for that, because he really did use it to flip a switch that had broken off.

Some things in this fictional book are fiction, though. Grace would probably not have survived launch in the lunar module because the power wasn't turned on in it yet. The astronauts did that after they entered. (Although maybe Ms. Tremt's beta scarf had even more powers than anyone imagined!) If Grace had turned the power on, she would have used up the oxygen the astronauts needed for their flight.

Also, in the real Apollo 11 mission, the astronauts boarded the command module before 7:00 a.m., not after 9:00 a.m. They also didn't have a group hallucination—at least, not as far as they ever told anyone.

The way the moon is described, including the way it looks and smells, does match what astronauts who have walked on the moon have said about it, though.

ERIK THORVALDSSON

Also known as Eric the Red, Erik Thorvaldsson was a Norwegian explorer who founded the first

European settlement on Greenland in 985 CE. He had four children, one of whom was Leif Eriksson, one of the first Europeans to reach North America. Erik got his nickname from his bright red hair and beard.

TRIEU THI TRINH

Trieu Thi Trinh has been called the Joan of Arc of Vietnam. Born around 225 CE, she raised an army of her own at the age of nineteen and took them to war against Chinese forces. She wore golden armor and rode an elephant, waving a sword in each hand as she led her troops into battle.

As one story says, when Trieu's brother told her to get married instead of becoming a warrior, she said, "I want to ride the storm, tame the waves, win back the fatherland, and destroy the yoke of slavery." She died in battle in 248 CE.

HYPATIA

Hypatia was a Greek woman who lived in Alexandria, Egypt, from 355–415 CE. Her father, a mathematician at the University of

Alexandria, taught her math, astronomy, and philosophy. She used what she learned to write and teach others. Hypatia wrote about advanced, difficult concepts in math and astronomy, and fought hard for her beliefs.

SIR ISAAC NEWTON

Sir Isaac Newton was one of the most important scientists who ever lived. (Even Albert Einstein said that Newton was the smartest person in history.) He developed the theory of gravity and the laws of motion that became the basis for physics. He also is responsible for creating a new type of mathematics, called calculus, and for inventing the reflecting telescope that is the model for nearly all the telescopes used in astronomy today.

Newton was born on a farm but lived at school for most of his life, until the Great Plague hit England in 1665. Then Newton had to return home to study for two years. He spent those years alone and worked on his most important theories during that period.

ALBERT EINSTEIN

Albert Einstein may have grown up to be one of the world's greatest scientific geniuses, but when he was a small boy, his grandmother said he was stupid! Einstein didn't talk until he was four years old, and until he was seven he would just repeat words and phrases over and over.

Einstein studied to be a teacher of math and physics. After he graduated, he moved to Switzerland and worked in the patent office in Bern. During his free time, he did thought experiments, where he tried to figure out the answers to complex problems. In 1915, Einstein proved his brilliance with his Theory of Relativity, which dealt with complex laws of physics.

Einstein's amazing brain wasn't so amazing at everything, though. He was famously disorganized and forgot appointments all the time. He never stopped using his imagination, though. Einstein said, "Imagination is more important than knowledge. For knowledge is limited to all we know and understand, while imagination embraces the entire world. . . ."

I like hanging out in the library after school, even though I don't study. I don't need to study, which I know sounds obnoxious, but I'm just really lucky. I inherited my mom's "elephant" memory (that's what she calls it—she hears or sees something once and then remembers it forever, and there's an old expression that says "an elephant never forgets"), so if I just listen in class and do my homework, I never have to actually sit down and study. Unlike my friend Ethan, who is sitting across from me right now, labeling the parts of a cell and doing it mostly wrong.

I sigh and continue playing MineFarm on my phone. I can correct him in a minute. A few weeks ago, Ethan asked me to tutor him after school, which I agreed to do, not only because he's a really good friend but also because the library is *quiet*, unlike my house, so being here is actually pleasant.

Ethan passes me his paper to look over, and I point out where he's mixed up different parts, as well as spelled "mitochondria" wrong.

Ethan groans. "Ava, if I didn't like you so much, I'd really *dis*like you. You get straight A's and you don't do *anything*."

"I know," I say. "I'm sorry. But I can't help having an elephant memory. Plus, I have my phone, so anything I *don't* know, I can just look up, and *poof*! There it is. Technology is a wonderful thing."

I bring my eyes back to my phone, where some zombies have gotten loose in my Mine-Farm game and are eating all of my cows. Shoot! I'll have to steal some of Ethan's cows, I guess. He always takes really good care of his farm. He's probably one of the best gamers I've ever played with.

Ethan must hear the sound of my cows being eaten because he pipes up, "Ava, don't even think about stealing my cows."

"Um, okay." I start to do it anyway.

Ethan is rewriting "mitochondria." "How'd you get this elephant memory anyway? Can I buy one at the mall?"

I smile. "Doubt it. I got it from my mom. When she was younger, she got into a really fancy college out in California but didn't end up going because she wanted to stay close to home. I can't believe it! If I had the chance to move to sunny California, I'd be there in a minute."

"To be closer to your dad?" Ethan asks.

My parents are divorced and my dad lives in Los Angeles now. My mom and my younger twin sisters and baby brother and I live here in the Northeast, and my mom works full-time, so there are always babysitters and missed meals and messes and laundry. Ugh. My house is a disaster. My dad lives alone and has a housekeeper, so in the summers when I go see him, it's like heaven.

"I'd like to live in California partly because of my dad, I guess," I tell Ethan. "But also because life is just *nicer* there. Haven't you seen the TV shows? It's warm and sunny all year, and there's less stress. Everyone is just hanging out outside. Everyone is happy there. It's the place to be."

I manage to steal about six of Ethan's cows, one at a time, and put them in my MineFarm cow pen. I turn the volume down on my phone so he doesn't hear me.

"I know what you just did," Ethan says as he starts to pack up his homework. "And you're cheating yourself, you know."

"Huh? I don't know what you're talking about," I say innocently.

"Stealing my cows! The fun of the game is in working hard and building your farm from scratch. And keeping it going, bit by bit, every day. But you just skip all that and take my animals. It's called *Mine*Farm, not *Yours*Farm."

Ethan laughs to himself, and I can't help laughing along with him. He knows me so well. It's nice to have a friend who will let you steal his cows and then really not even care about it. *And* make stupid jokes about it.

As I'm looking at Ethan, I see something *very weird* out the window behind him. It's an actual cow. Like, a real, live cow. And it's looking at me.

I start laughing really hard. "Hey, Ethan. Don't have a cow, but—"

Ethan shakes his head. "I'm not having a cow. I'm actually being very cool about the fact that you constantly steal supplies from me and I still play with you."

"No, no," I say. "Look, there's a cow right there, out the window! In the school yard! A real cow!" I point over his head, and Ethan turns around and sees it.

"That is a real dairy cow," Ethan says. "Holy cow. Holy COW! And is that . . . ?"

I nod my head. Not that it wasn't already weird enough, but our school's librarian, Ms. Tremt, is now outside patting the cow and trying to lead it away from the front of the school.

"I'm going to go help her!" Ethan says, jumping up. He runs toward the side exit door of the library and is outside in just a moment. I can't believe what I'm seeing, but it looks like Ms. Tremt and Ethan are talking to the cow, trying to verbally convince it to go somewhere. Of course, it looks like it weighs about two tons, so good luck to them.

Ethan looks through the window at me and throws up his hands. He clearly thinks Ms. Tremt is a bit batty. Then he tries clapping and calling to the cow like he would call to a dog. Surprise, surprise—that doesn't work either.

I shake my head at their ridiculousness and do a quick search on "how to move a cow" on my phone. Technology. Seriously. It's the best.

The answer pops up in less than three seconds, and I start digging in my lunch bag for my leftovers. As soon as I have something in my hand, I go outside and walk straight up to the cow.

I can hear Ms. Tremt talking now. "What if somebody sees you?" she tells the cow. "You could fall into the wrong hands! You can't just take the situation into your own hooves, you know."

I give the cow a piece of the carrot I'm holding, then begin walking away, holding more of the carrot. The cow follows me, as easy as one, two, three. Thanks, Internet! You've saved the day, for the billionth time.

"Well done, Ava," Ms. Tremt says. "You have a real way with animals. Now, could you please lead your new friend into the back room of the library for me?"

I look from her to Ethan and back to her. "Uh, Ms. Tremt? Shouldn't we call animal control or something? Or the ASPCA? Or, um, a vet? My mom works as a vet. I could call her."

Ms. Tremt smiles broadly at me, then uses her lime-green fuzzy scarf to point in the direction of the side door to the library. "That won't be nec-essary, Ava. But thank you for your suggestions. Just take Ms. Cow to the back room."

I do as she asks, because even a kooky grown-up is still a grown-up, but I exchange more than a few looks with Ethan while doing it. All I can think about is how big of a mess that cow is going to make when it goes to the bathroom in the middle of the school's library. Maybe Ethan and I will have to study at his house tomorrow after school.

As soon as the cow is settled in the back room with Ms. Tremt, I go to gather up my things. My phone beeps that it's five thirty p.m., and I realize how late I've stayed. "I've got to get home," I tell Ethan.

He nods and helps me pack up. "Oh, yeah! I forgot it was your big night, right?"

I roll my eyes. "My big night" is just the night that my mom's and my favorite TV show, *World's Weirdest Animals*, comes on. "Exactly. So I need to jet. Are you coming?"

Ethan shakes his head. "Nah, not yet. Ms. Tremt asked me to come to her office and help her with something real quick before I go. But I'll see you later on MineFarm. I've got to start breeding more cows, apparently."

I laugh and wave good-bye, then head out the side door again, this time to the bike rack where my scooter is locked up. There are a few kids grabbing bikes, and I wait a moment before I push in to get my scooter.

Once I have it unlocked, I send a quick text to my mom to let her know I'm leaving school and will be home in seven minutes. As I'm sliding my phone into my backpack, someone slams into me, and a bunch of my homework papers explode out of my bag and fly all over the ground.

Ugh. I bend to pick them up, and as I do, I see it was a Viking—yes, a *Viking*—that slammed into me. He's wearing metal armor and a horned helmet and everything.

"Um, hello?" I say.

He grunts, and to my surprise, starts helping me to pick up the papers. He hands me a stack, then says, "Many hands make light work."

Quick as lightning, I put the two very weird

things that have happened that day together. "You wouldn't happen to own a cow, would you?" I ask.

He narrows his eyes. "Yes, I do. In fact, all cows are my cows."

Hmm. This just got weirder. I decide to leave the, uh, *Viking* and the cow situation in Ms. Tremt's capable hands. I figure she'll know what to do. Weird things always seem to be happening in the library and around Ms. Tremt, now that I think about it. I turn back to the Viking. "Um, okay. Gotta go!"

I hop on my scooter and sail home. Hopefully it will be less chaotic than this afternoon in the library was. But I doubt it.

Do you love zany adventures, laugh-out-loud situations, and crazy fun stories? Then you'll love reading about Kid inventor Billy Sure in

BILLY SURE
· KID ENTREPRENEUR ·